LIES WE KEEP

A PIECES OF ME NOVEL
BOOK ONE

DANIELLE ROSE

LIES WE KEEP

A PIECES OF ME NOVEL
BOOK ONE

DANIELLE ROSE

WATERHOUSE PRESS

For Tara, Francie, and Brittany—

You're my real-life inspirations behind one helluva friend. I love you all.

CHAPTER ONE

I leaned against the window and stared at the busy streets below. From this elevation, the world consisted of grids, each square block perfectly aligned with the next. A rigid structure designed to keep everything in place. It reminded me of my current situation.

I had signed with a new publisher who had requested I suddenly transform myself from a pantser—an organic writer who simply goes with the flow—to a plotter, where everything is carefully laid out and planned. But my writing process wasn't like these seemingly perfect Manhattan streets. Much like my life, it was messy and often out of sequence.

I'd told my new publisher I could do it. I could become the plotting fool they wished me to be. But that promise, like this view of Manhattan, was a lie.

I took a swig of coffee from my to-go cup and smiled. I loved Manhattan—the people, the smells, the food, the shops. I had an explicit love affair with the city, and I wasn't afraid to admit it. There was a hum to it, a hustle and bustle seen nowhere else.

"Three more for today," Tara said from across her office.

"Huh?" I turned to face my best friend and literary agent as she glanced at the clock on the wall, her long, black locks swaying as she frantically gathered paperwork.

"Three more interviews, Jez."

"Ah, right." I'd forgotten I'd asked her a question.

Tara had set up a number of appointments to interview candidates for a position I'd never dreamed I'd have an opening for. A bodyguard.

When I started writing romance novels, I didn't realize how drastically my life would change. The men I dated suddenly expected me to act like the porn-star wannabes in my novels, and it became so annoying that it drained me to the point of celibacy. I wasn't proud of it, and I was even less proud of the number of batteries Mr. Dependable had gone through in recent months.

But lack of sex wasn't the worst part. Fame came with other consequences—the kind celebrity magazines often showcased. My number of admirers was staggering, and many had professed a particularly worrying form of *deep* devotion. These stalkers could be grabby at times, but they were usually harmless. Usually.

Two years ago, my debut novel had been published to widespread acclaim. A year after that, it had reached Hollywood. Six months ago, the letters began. And this wasn't ordinary fan mail. They were detailed accounts of what would happen if he and I ever met.

He sent me drawings of women in submissive positions. And this wasn't your typical consensual spanking, hair pulling, blindfolds, and handcuffs. The way he described his fantasies, the way he outlined the women in his drawings, was...unnerving.

After reading the first threatening letter, Tara—and even the police—suggested I relocate far, far away. Plucking away on an antique typewriter on the front porch of a log cabin surrounded by acres of lakes and mountains was a trope movies used to beautify this industry. In my reality, being a writer was already a lonely—if not quite as picturesque— profession.

I might be stubborn and stupid, but I wasn't about to leave Manhattan for *any* reason. Chances were, it's the only soul mate I'd find. I wasn't leaving it behind.

So Tara had looked for other ways to keep me safe, which included possibly hiring a person to do it. While I had been concerned about the letters, I never considered their sender to be a serious threat. Hiring a bodyguard seemed like overkill.

But here I was, interviewing bodyguards, dressed in skinny black-leather jeans and my favorite off-the-shoulder cashmere sweater that hugged my hips. Tara had begged me to take the formal-attire approach, but I didn't see the point. The person I was hoping to hire today would see me at my best, worst, and most casual. None of which would be me in a suit.

I watched Tara's reflection in the floor-to-ceiling windows that boxed in her corner office. Unlike me, she *did* take the formal approach. She often dressed in bright colors to contrast with her smooth, dark skin. Today, she'd chosen gray slacks and a bright-blue blouse. I was envious of her ability to look truly fantastic in the boldest of colors. I couldn't pull off such daring looks.

In addition to her fashion sense, I'd also always admired her work ethic. Like me, she put her job before anything else, and it showed.

Either Tara could sell an idea for top dollar or she couldn't. Clearly, she could. Either I could write or I couldn't. Clearly, I could. And when Tara realized I could, she signed me as her first client. Together, we got her this corner office.

Three more interviews. I stifled a groan. I knew I needed to be here, to do this. With each passing day, he, she, whoever it was, was sending more letters and getting closer, but we were no closer to finding a good bodyguard, and I was cranky.

And hungry.

That was a lethal combination—especially for a writer. I was one pen stroke away from killing off someone in my next book. And I was supposed to write love stories.

I sipped my coffee and looked back down at my fellow New Yorkers scurrying about, desperately trying to make it wherever they were going on time and in one piece. From my viewpoint, they were nothing but ants on the hunt, taking orders from their queen. I blinked, and the group I'd been spying on disappeared through traffic.

I wondered if this stalker was there, watching me watch them. Could he see me up here?

A quick knock against the door brought me back to reality, and I spun on my heel to greet the intruder.

"Come in," Tara said as she gathered her clipboard. She glanced at me, giving her best reassuring smile.

"Mrs. Johnson," Tara's assistant said, "Mr. James Blakely is here for his interview."

She stepped aside, and the finest male specimen I'd ever set eyes upon strode in. My breath caught. He was delicious.

His dark-gray suit was tailored to perfection and strained around his thighs as he walked toward us. My eyes trailed the length of his body, from his large black shoes to his long legs to his lean torso. His chiseled jaw held a five o'clock shadow, and his brown hair was cropped perfectly.

I, without a doubt, would be fucking him in my dreams tonight.

At the very least, he would inspire my latest heroine's next love interest. With each step he took, I could feel the confining layers of writer's block being stripped away.

He offered his hand to Tara, who muffled a greeting,

seemingly unaware of what had just stumbled into her office.

That was what married life did to you, and for the first time in months, I was glad her single-radar was broken.

Because the moment Mr. James Blakely walked into her office, he was *mine.*

When he grasped my hand, his eyes softened, even though I was sure he'd noticed me eye-fucking him. He was probably used to it. A man like this commanded any room he walked into. The testosterone flowed from him in waves, slamming into me and nearly bringing me to my knees. He was an alpha male, through and through. I, too, was a proud alpha. Submissive wasn't in my dictionary.

But I'd be lying if I said the thought of being tied up and spanked by this man didn't cross my mind in a flash.

I suppose the real question was, could he handle an alpha female?

I knew what I wanted, and I wasn't afraid to take it. That intimidated most men. I silently prayed to whatever god or goddess would listen that this man wouldn't know the meaning of intimidation.

And until I could *take him*, Mr. Dependable would be putting in overtime to images of this sexual fiend.

I stared, unwilling to release him from my grasp. He stood just a foot away. His scent lingered, tickling my nose. He smelled of cologne, mint, and the undeniable scent of a god. My favorite smell. I inhaled slowly, licking my lips.

His eyes dropped, watching as my tongue slowly escaped back into my mouth and my teeth dragged against the skin of my lower lip. Other than the drop of his eyes and the tiny muscles clenching in his jaw, betraying his control, he showed no signs of weakness.

I was going to have to work hard for this one. And I was completely okay with that.

It wasn't every day I met someone I'd shamelessly fuck into oblivion, and it definitely wasn't every day that I met someone who could handle the demanding role of my heroine's love interest.

Even so, internally, I pouted. But what did I expect? He sure wasn't going to toss me over his shoulder, slam me down on Tara's desk, and fuck me until the entire building knew his name.

I made a mental note to get my own office for such an occasion.

The firm lines of his lips softened until a crooked, sly smile formed. That smile said everything. It told me he knew *exactly* what I was thinking.

Fuck, I wanted this man. Badly.

It had been months—*months*—since I'd been with someone other than Mr. Dependable. I fought the urge to rip off his clothes and mount him like the stallion he clearly was.

Tara cleared her throat, and I tore my eyes away from Mr. Sex God's. In my moment of weakness, I hadn't realized Tara had already taken her seat. She stared awkwardly and fidgeted with invisible lint on her pants.

Only then did I realize I still held his hand. Playing it cool, I shrugged, dropping his hand and stepping back, needing the safety space provided before I jumped him.

"Thanks for coming, Mr. Blakely," I said with a small smile as I took my seat beside Tara.

With wall-to-wall windows, Tara's office had always felt large. Now, as Blakely took his seat and casually rested his hands on his lap, it felt too intimate. The usual open, breezy atmosphere was no more, and silently, as Tara flipped through her papers, I wondered if my not-so-subtle fawning was as obvious as I assumed it had been.

Who was I kidding? Of course it was. I was sure even Tara's assistant, who hadn't stayed to watch our interaction, knew what took place.

The catcall of a woman in heat could be heard for miles.

"Thank you for considering me, Miss Tate. While I'm sorry to say I haven't personally read your books, your reputation precedes you. It's an honor to simply be interviewed."

His voice was deep, smooth, and it washed over me in ecstatic waves. Was it even possible for him to get any sexier?

"You're not exactly my target audience." I winked. Had I seriously just done that? Internally, I rolled my eyes at myself. *Get it together, Jez!*

He clenched his jaw, the defined muscles tightening. The area between my legs quivered. There was nothing sexier than a man with a chiseled jaw who happened to be wearing a suit. I had every cologne, luxury car, and evening wear commercial to thank for my high expectations of a man's appearance.

"Right, so," Tara said, tapping the end of her pencil against her notepad, "tell us a little about yourself, Mr. Blakely."

"I enlisted in the Marine Corps at seventeen, but shortly after, I was placed in a special operative team. Last year, when it came time to renew my contract, I left."

"Why is that?" Tara asked.

He swallowed, his Adam's apple bouncing against his throat.

I held back a moan. Since when did I find Adam's apples sexy?

"My unit wanted out, and I was loyal to them. It was time

for them to retire. They'd already put in twenty years, and they had spouses, children. With the rest leaving, I didn't feel the need to stay. To be frank, I wasn't interested in joining another team."

"Loyalty's important," Tara stated.

"It is, ma'am."

Our eyes locked, and I saw it. The emptiness. The alpha stripped away. The man who sat before me wasn't the cool, collected person he'd been showing us. He was damaged, wounded. He blinked, and it was gone; the facade returned. The switch was brief, lingering just long enough for me to see myself in him.

"Do you have family?" I asked, swallowing the knot that formed in my throat whenever I allowed my memories to creep into my conscious.

He arched an eyebrow. After my earlier display, he probably assumed there was a hidden meaning to my question.

But he was wrong.

Scratch away the surface, the pretty face, the muscular body, and I saw the vulnerability that he tried to hide in his eyes. There was darkness there. And I knew it well.

I saw that same sadness every time I looked in the mirror.

"No, ma'am," he said simply. His lack of an elaboration told me everything I needed to know. I'd given the same quick responses and generic replies whenever someone asked me about my family.

Few people could be asked that question and honestly answer with a "no."

I was one of those people, and clearly, Blakely was, too.

I released a long breath. "Please, call me Jezebel."

"Jez means to say that this job requires a lot."

I knew Tara would chime in. She was more than just my agent or my friend. After the accident that claimed my parents' lives, she strove to be my savior.

"It's twenty-four-seven, three-sixty-five work. You'll be staying at Jez's apartment. At least until things settle. This would be taxing on a significant other or any children. I imagine you'd hate the position after just a few weeks."

"Understandable, of course, but no, I don't have anyone. Being in the military for the past fourteen years made it impossible to form relationships, and my parents died when I was young. They didn't have siblings. I've been on my own for years."

Tara offered a sad smile. "I'm sorry, Mr. Blakely."

He brushed away her concern with the wave of his hand. "It's been a long time."

I shifted in my chair, wondering how long it'd take until I could shrug away concern with that same ease. The conversation had taken a turn for the worse—a turn I'd instigated. The familiarity of his words was too close for comfort. That longing he showed mirrored my own—and I wasn't ready to deal with those feelings yet.

I wasn't sure I'd ever be ready to deal with the death of my parents—or the fact that I'd been responsible.

I cleared my throat, and Tara understood my silent message. I chastised myself for succumbing to the past. The past hurt, but I couldn't change it. I needed to live for now. I pushed down the pain and focused on the interview, focused on Blakely.

That brief vulnerability I'd witnessed in his eyes was gone. I could do the same.

"Can you tell us about any specialized training you've

had?" Tara asked quickly, giving me something to focus on.

He nodded, but as he answered her question, his eyes were on me, acknowledging the way I shifted uncomfortably. He acted just like a bodyguard. He was already annoyingly good at it, and I hadn't even hired him yet.

"I've studied various forms of martial arts, though I'm passionate about Krav Maga. It focuses more on you and your surroundings. I'm much more about having a good offense than defense. Certain situations are avoidable. It just depends on how you work the people around you. I'm very good at reading people," he said, his eyes still on me.

"Great. Anything else?" Tara asked.

At some point, I would have to speak again. I knew this. I was just finding it incredibly difficult to put even simple thoughts together. My primal instincts, though, were clearly intact.

My emotions were waging a war within me. I was torn between fight or flight—or just screwing the man in front of me.

"I've taken up boxing, and staying fit and healthy has always been important to me—even before I joined the military. I've also been trained to handle various weapons, and I have a concealed-carry permit."

I tried to focus on my potential bodyguard. His arms strained against the fabric of his suit as he leaned forward and adjusted in his seat. I met his gaze, and he smiled. I swallowed down the drool that would have inevitably slid down my chin. Was I having the same effect on him? He gave away nothing.

"Have you ever been a bodyguard?" I asked.

"In a way, yes. Since leaving the military, I've been working odd jobs that've required me to run security for...individuals during events."

I nodded. "Anyone I know?"

"Perhaps."

He didn't elaborate, and I didn't push it further. Most of his clients were likely wealthy and paid him good money to keep his mouth shut. Just like I would if I were to hire him. He was going to see me at my best and worst, and I needed to know that he could keep his experiences confidential. Sure, if he was hired, he'd have to sign the dotted line that told him to shut up, but I liked to know there was more there. I liked to know his silence was more than just a thin piece of paper between him and whoever bid the highest for my baggage.

"Well, this all sounds great. We have a few more interviews lined up, but once we make our decision, we'll—"

"I want him," I said. I knew those words held a deeper meaning, and I was sure he knew it, too.

But this wasn't about the burning desire to rip off his clothes. This was the first candidate I cared to be around, and his background was more than sufficient. I knew Tara would recommend him once he left the room—so I beat her to it.

"Excuse me?" Tara whispered.

Tara had always been by the book. She liked order; I liked emotion. Every decision I made was emotion-based. It might not have been the best strategy at times, but I was still breathing.

"You're hired," I said, ignoring Tara.

"Jez, we still need to run background checks and—"

"Then you're hired as soon as you pass the background checks."

Tara frowned. We hadn't discussed this, and I knew that bothered her. But the truth was, I was going to spend a lot of time with this person. I'd rather have that person be someone I was comfortable being around.

And, really, I wanted to fuck the guy. Could I feel any more comfortable around him than that?

"Tara, someone thought it was a good idea to hand him a gun permit, so I'm fairly confident he's safe."

"Jeze—"

"How long will it take to get the background checks in?" I asked.

"Well, we can rush them," she replied.

I nodded and leaned over, grabbing the folder that lay on Tara's lap.

"Has he signed a nondisclosure yet?" I asked as I flipped through the documents in the folder.

"Yes, ma'am, I have," he said when I reached the stack of stapled documents I'd been looking for. I tugged it from the folder and handed it to him. He scanned it as I spoke.

"This lists your pay, benefits, and what would be expected of you. Take some time to read it thoroughly, and give me an answer once your background checks come back."

He frowned.

"What is it?" I asked.

"The pay." He glanced up. "This is too much."

I shook my head. "I pay well."

"I can't accept this."

I cleared my throat and stepped into my business shoes— the ones I loathed wearing because they hurt like a bitch. "This isn't a gift, Mr. Blakely. The person I hire will be uprooting. The person I hire will have little to no social life. The person I hire must be willing to take a bullet for me. I don't look at my expectations lightly, so what I pay is fair. I should warn you, though, before you get to the next page. There are pay increases after certain milestones. If you stay with me for a long time, you very likely will become a rich man."

"I have no desire to be rich," he said. "Money changes people."

I blinked once. Twice. He was right. Money did change people, and usually, it wasn't for the better. Even so, I hadn't expected that response.

He swallowed hard, his Adam's apple bobbing deliciously in his throat. "I— I apologize, ma'am. That was uncalled for and unacceptable. It won't happen again."

I brushed away his concern. "No worries. I didn't take it personally. So, we'll be in touch?"

He smiled. "Yes, ma'am."

I gestured for the packet. "Give me that packet back."

He frowned but handed it over.

Unclipping the pen from Tara's clipboard, I flipped to the back page, scribbled something down, and handed the papers back to him.

He grinned as he read what I'd written.

"What did you add?" Tara asked.

"Another condition of employment. This 'ma'am' business won't work. I'm twenty-seven, Mr. Blakely, not seventy-two."

He flashed a wide, cheeky grin, and I nearly swooned.

"Well, Mr. Blakely, we have your paperwork, and we'll process your background checks. We'll be in touch in a day or so," Tara said.

He nodded and stood. "Thank you," he said, shaking her hand.

I absently handed Tara her folder and pen as I shook his hand. His blue eyes sparkled as they searched mine.

"Until we meet again, Mr. Blakely," I promised. His name

rolled around my head, and I couldn't deny that I liked the sound of it.

I reached the door that held us captive in Tara's office and yanked it open. The cool air of the hallway assaulted me, and only then did I realize I'd been overheated. My porcelain skin was likely pink, made even brighter by the light gray of my sweater. I cringed at the thought.

I turned back and brushed up against my soon-to-be bodyguard's firm torso. He caught my hand before I could tumble into him, steadying me. I bit my lip as I glanced up. He was tall. Very tall. I hadn't noticed earlier. I was five foot seven, but in my black pumps, I was pushing five foot ten. He still towered over me—a good half-foot, at least. Realizing I was already practically groping my hired help, I stepped back and ran a hand through my hair to brush away the chocolate-brown strands that fell before my eyes.

"Tara will put a rush on the checks." *Because I'd like to make sure I'm not fucking a sociopath.*

I glanced at her. She nodded in response, still sitting in her chair.

Blakely nodded and smiled as he passed me. I bit my lip and rested against the doorframe as I watched his retreat, my eyes trailing the length of his torso, stopping when they reached his perfect ass. I sighed.

He pushed the button for the elevator, walked in, and then kept his eyes on me until the doors closed.

This one was going to be trouble.

CHAPTER TWO

I slid my key into the lock, listening for the familiar clunk. I turned and waved to the overly friendly taxi driver, who insisted on waiting until I was safely within the confines of my Upper West Side brownstone. I closed the door behind me and took the stairs to my third-floor apartment.

My building was easy to spot. It was the only brownstone on the block that had been painted white. The contrast of the white brick beside the endless rows of red and brown brick was jarring.

I still remembered the day I moved into my apartment. The building had been brown then, and the interior was dark to match. I bulldozed through the entire apartment and started from scratch, creating a beautiful open-concept retreat. And now, the bright whites and light grays of my apartment matched the outside brick.

Painting the brownstone had been the talk of the neighborhood. The building was in a historic district that was known for its brownstones, so naturally, painting and modernizing the building was considered taboo. I was sure there were rules in place to prevent this from happening, but money talked. Someone along the way paid off someone else to look the other way, and now, I lived in a white brownstone.

A whitestone.

It just didn't have the same ring to it.

Eventually, people got over it, and I could grab my mail in

peace without hearing about our white bricks. We went back to the usual relationships between New Yorkers.

In truth, we never spoke. Not anymore.

I closed the front door to my apartment and latched the five locks that separated the rest of the world from me. The chain, deadbolt, and doorknob lock weren't enough, I'd learned, after a close encounter. I'd been staying at a hotel while my apartment was being painted, and I came back to my hotel room one day to find it ransacked. My underwear and bras had been placed delicately on the bedspread, as if the intruder wanted me to know he'd been sniffing my panties. Even with the hotel's security staff, cameras, and a locked door, he'd still managed to get in.

To give Tara peace of mind, I'd added two extra deadbolts to my apartment door. Each lock had a different key, which meant it took me several minutes just to get through my front door. I didn't know how to pick a lock. Maybe having a different key for each lock didn't even matter. But it made Tara and me feel better.

Luckily, my apartment took up the entire third floor, which meant no one was taking that extra flight of stairs unless they were coming to see me.

Having the upper level also meant I was the only one with access to the rooftop deck—just like the first-floor apartment had access to the garden out back. The only thing the occupant of the second-floor apartment got was cheaper rent.

The lady who lived there was a shut-in. Our first-floor neighbor used to bring her baked treats, but now she didn't open the door for anyone. In fact, I didn't think she opened the door at all. After she'd stopped answering phone calls, the baked goods were left outside her door. They sat there until they molded and the building's superintendent tossed them.

She stopped receiving much of anything after that. I guess she wanted to escape reality. She wanted to be left alone.

I could relate to that.

I dropped my bag onto my kitchen counter and strolled into my living room. I drew back the curtains to let in the light and smiled. The street was bumper-to-bumper with cars. I didn't understand why anyone had a car in Manhattan. Between gas prices, insurance premiums, parking fees, and the readily available public transportation, the decision to go green had been easy for me.

I stood back and scanned the room, which served as my living room, dining room, and, since I'd cleared out the spare bedroom for the bodyguard, office. Though open, it felt cluttered with my desk in the room. I liked having it open and airy, especially since there wasn't much space when I ventured outside. My style was modern minimalist, so even when I looked for items to toss to make room, I couldn't let go of anything. Everything I owned had a purpose.

My phone buzzed in my bag on the kitchen counter. I dug it out and glanced at the screen to find a picture of Tara and a flashing text message icon.

Background checks sent.

I smiled. I hadn't thought about Blakely after he'd left, but I was sure I'd be thinking about him tonight. I texted Tara back.

Thanks. Keep me updated.

She replied instantly.

Will do.

I tossed my phone onto the counter and walked past the kitchen and down the hall. The apartment's one bathroom was to my left, and at the end of the hall were two bedrooms. I walked into the spare, crossing my arms and looking around.

"Seems...empty," I said aloud.

After I had moved my desk to the living room, I'd furnished the room with a bed, end tables, and a dresser. But that was it. The room was lifeless. The bed was bare, the closets were empty, and I hadn't yet gotten lamps.

I squealed and ran back into the kitchen. I grabbed my phone and quickly texted Tara.

Shopping?

I glanced at the time. Eleven thirty a.m.

And lunch?

While I waited, I scanned my emails. Every day, I woke to even more that Tara had forwarded to me from the press. I rolled my eyes and deleted them without reading. The press was so demanding and, by far, the worst part of being a writer.

Prior to moving into my apartment, they'd discovered where I lived and stalked me. I'd wake to reporters at my door every morning, and I'd come home to them every evening. A girl could only provide so many statements.

I searched my weather app. It had been cooler earlier, but soon the heat of the afternoon's sun would be suffocating. The air would turn humid, muggy. My black-leather pants and sweater would be too heavy. I silently chastised my wardrobe choice. After all, it was June in New York. What was I thinking?

I padded into my bedroom, stripped off my clothes, and stepped into my walk-in closet.

One by one, I searched through the garments until I settled on a pair of shorts and a dark-gray camisole. I slid sandals on my feet and left my bedroom, knotting my thick hair into a messy bun.

I grabbed a bottle of water from my fridge and plopped down at the counter bar. My phone's screen lit up.

Meeting. Sorry!

I frowned and stuffed my water bottle and cell phone into my bag.

Maybe I could go alone.

Was that idea stupid? Careless? After all, I had promised to work harder at taking this threat more seriously.

I turned in my seat, staring at my front door. I tried to recall the last time I had received a letter from him. It'd been a couple of weeks since he'd last made contact.

Maybe he'd given up.

Maybe I was finally free.

CHAPTER THREE

I stumbled onto the street, hiking the strap of my purse up onto my shoulder. Six hours had passed, and I still hadn't heard back from Tara about Blakely's background checks. I was sure that was normal, but even so, I was getting anxious. We'd had the checks rushed, but what did that mean? How long would it take to get a rushed check back?

The heels of my sandals clunked against the concrete as I juggled the shopping bags in my hands. I may have gone a little overboard, but I couldn't pass up a good sale. As I walked back toward my apartment, I window-shopped, taking mental notes of stores I'd return to once I had a lighter load.

I couldn't remember the last time I felt this alive. I felt free, invisible...safe.

Maybe it was just a nightmare.

Maybe it was just a joke.

Or maybe it was over...

I hadn't been paying attention, and I'd nearly run into another shopper. When my eyes locked with his, I stopped short.

"Blakely," I said, surprised.

His sapphire eyes sparkled in the sunlight.

"Miss Tate." His tone was stern as he glanced around, concern etching his eyes. "Are you shopping alone?"

"Yes."

His eyes narrowed. "Is that wise? You're hiring a bodyguard."

Suddenly, I felt ridiculous, because he was right. How could I have been this naïve? The heroines from my novels would have never acted as reckless—and they certainly wouldn't have needed a man to chastise such behavior.

"You're just worried about job security." I laughed, finding myself, once again, trying to play it cool around him. Who had I become? A high schooler?

I hadn't noticed his less-than-formal attire. Wearing only jeans and a T-shirt, James Blakely was just as drop-dead gorgeous as he had been this morning. The scruff on his chin and the mess of his hair only added to his casual style. A sheer layer of sweat dampened his skin. Biting my lip, I imagined him working out—all sweaty, breathing heavily, looking completely fuckable. And I'd thought he was sexy in a suit...

"Everything about you concerns me," he said, and I felt the words hit my core.

I shifted uncomfortably. Was this going to work? How could I *live* with him? I could barely keep control on a street corner.

"Let me help you with your bags," he said, offering his hands. "Where are you parked?"

I shook my head. "It's okay. I'm walking."

He arched an eyebrow. "Walking?"

I nodded.

The seconds ticked by as he stared at me. In the time that passed before he spoke, I could have written the next bestseller. Just as I was contemplating the title, he smiled. "I can see I'll have my work cut out for me."

I returned his smile. "You mean *if* you get the job, right?"

"Yeah, *if* I get the job," he said sarcastically.

"You don't seem worried," I said.

He shook his head. "You're waiting on my background checks. I already know what those will tell you."

My body was only inches away from his. To onlookers, we likely looked like two people in love, about to kiss, but in reality, a storm of emotions passed through me.

What I wouldn't give to drop my bags, wrap my arms around his neck, and press my lips against his...

"I'd like to walk you home," he said, his eyes dropping to my lips.

His words said everything yet nothing. Empty promises. A dangerous vow to what he would and wouldn't do.

I wasn't sure what I appreciated more—his control or his temperament.

"If you were my bodyguard, what would you think if I told you I let some strange man walk me home?" I was teasing him, and I was sure he liked it.

He smiled.

"Like you said, we're still waiting on those checks," I added.

His eyes said everything his mouth wouldn't.

My breath caught, and I was sure he heard it. The gasp, the wonder, the promise, it resonated deep within me—and made my panties wet. I dragged my teeth against the skin of my bottom lip and relished in watching his eyes turn dark as they lingered on that spot.

His jaw clenched as he lowered his head toward mine. I angled upward, and our lips brushed. The familiar scent of his musk surrounded me, teasing my senses. My knees grew weak, and I was sure, at any moment, I'd topple to the ground. I leaned into him. My breasts rubbed against his shirt, and my nipples peaked at the electric static that coursed between us. A low rumble worked its way up his chest in response, and I felt myself smile inside. He reached around, placing a hand at the small of my back. My camisole had ridden up, and his thumb teased the skin there, rubbing softly. My eyes fluttered shut as I waited for him to make the next move.

Only he didn't.

I opened my eyes, and in that instant, the world changed, flipping on its head. He pulled away, clearing his throat. He stepped back several paces and ran a hand through his hair.

"I should call you a taxi," he said as he turned.

What the fuck was that?

Angry, bitter, rejected, and horny, I took the child's way out.

"I don't want a damn taxi," I said as I stomped down the street toward my apartment.

I heard him groan just before I felt him grab my arm and pull me to a stop.

"I'm sorry," he said.

I shrugged. "Don't be. I'm not."

I yanked my arm free and continued walking down the street. I was making a scene, but I didn't care. That was the beauty of living in Manhattan. No one cared about you. I was in a swarm of people, yet only Blakely saw me. That was what I loved about this city.

I was invisible.

I hadn't noticed he was following me until someone cut in front of me and I came to an abrupt stop. Blakely walked into me, his hands falling to my arms as he tried to balance us both.

I could get used to these meetings.

Every inch of his frame was pressed against mine. Every rigid muscle of him pressed firmly against the soft curves of my body. My hands fell to my sides, the bags dropping into piles on the ground, as the curve of my ass rubbed against his hardening length. He pressed his nose into my hair. He inhaled deeply, taking in my scent.

He wanted me. Here. Now.

The effect he had on me was no different than the effect I had on him.

I smiled and pulled away, turning to face him.

His eyes betrayed the carnal need ravishing him, but when he blinked, it was gone.

Seducing him was easy. Breaking through his self-control would be the fight of my life.

But I promised myself I'd have him.

Naked. Sweaty. Hard. Moaning. Beneath me.

I'd have him.

He bent over, grabbed my bags, and carried them in silence to my apartment. When we reached the top floor, we filed in, and I told him to drop them on the kitchen counter.

I texted Tara.

Any news yet?

"Want a tour?" I asked Blakely as I tucked my phone in my pocket.

"Sure," he said.

I turned on my heel. "Well, this is pretty much it. Living room, dining area, and office." I pointed to each space. "That door in the corner leads to the rooftop deck."

"You're the only one with access to that?" he asked, walking into the living room.

"Yep. It's all mine."

He nodded, his eyes scanning the space like he was taking mental notes.

I suddenly felt a wave of self-consciousness erupt within me, and I followed his gaze. I saw my apartment every day, but now, I looked at the room as if I were seeing it for the first time, envisioning what he must be seeing. The room was tidy, but this wasn't unusual. I had more than enough "neat" to accompany my "freak" in the personality department. Plus, my modern-minimalist style didn't allow for clutter. Even so, I wondered why I cared. I doubted he had strong feelings toward decor. Sure, he probably didn't want to live with a slob, because who did? But there was something more here.

I *cared* about his opinion. What was he thinking now? He stared at one of the oversized paintings that decorated my walls, tilting his head as he took in the splashes of color.

"It's mine," I said softly.

Looking back at me, he arched a brow. "You paint?"

I shrugged. "Not professionally." I hesitated before quietly adding, "Obviously."

"I think it's great." He smiled.

I felt my cheeks heat as I thanked him and looked at the painting. I'd painted it after the accident. It was a modern piece. To the untrained eye, I'm sure it looked like just a slop of paint on canvas, but to me, it was so much more. Each delicate stroke had a purpose. I'd mixed dark colors—blues, purples, greens, and grays—and added metallic hues where I saw fit. It was chaos, a perfect representation of the person inside, of the woman I became after that day. It wasn't until months later that I saw the light hidden within it. There were small splashes of bright metallic blue that looked almost white at their centers. It was as if the brightness was trying to shine through.

Few had seen my artwork. Most focused solely on my written words. And I was okay with that because I was learning that too much attention brought despair.

Was that why I'd felt so...vulnerable? This wasn't the first time others had invaded my personal space, but never in all my years of being the center of attention did the thought elicit my skin to flush, my stomach to tremble, and my heart to skip a beat.

I thought that was only for the romance novels I penned late at night.

"The bedrooms are through there?" he asked, signaling toward the lone hallway by the front door.

I nodded, turned back, and continued the tour. "Kitchen. Island. Bar stools." I walked down the hallway and stopped midway, opening a door. "Laundry."

I closed the door and continued walking until we reached the end alcove.

I turned to my left. "The one and only bathroom and"—I turned back toward my right—"the two bedrooms. Mine's on the right. Yours is on the left."

I glanced up at him and found him watching me intently. I arched an eyebrow and walked into his room. He followed closely behind me.

"That's why I was shopping. The room feels...empty. I picked up bedsheets, two bedside lamps, and a rug for here," I said, pointing to the space between the bed and the dresser.

He looked around, nodding.

"What do you think?" I asked.

"It's nice. Big."

I nodded. "Yeah, the apartment is a pretty decent size for being a shared brownstone."

"How many people live in this building?"

"Well, there are three levels. A recluse of a woman lives on the second floor. Never even leaves. And a family of four lives on the first floor. I don't know them, though."

His eyes met mine. "Why not?"

"They're new."

"How long have they lived here?"

I shrugged. "I don't know. A month?"

He nodded. "I'll look into it."

"You do that, Mr. Bodyguard."

He smiled and walked around the room, taking in what would be his new home if his background checks cleared, and Lord knew I'd been praying for that since the moment we'd met.

"Is it what you were expecting?" I asked, feeling slightly self-conscious.

He faced me. "Nothing about you has been what I was expecting."

Tell me about it.

"Hungry?" I asked, changing the subject.

His eyes darkened, and a mischievous smile crossed his lips as he said, "Very."

I stepped forward, eliminating the space between us. I placed my palms against his chest, his heart sputtering quickly beneath them, and stood on my tiptoes. His eyes widened. I was sure my boldness surprised us both.

If he wanted to play games, then so would I. I liked to tease. He'd figure that out the hard way.

My cheek rested against the stubble of his jaw, and my lips grazed his neck. I listened as he inhaled quickly and held the breath. Ever so lightly, I blew on his earlobe and bit my lip as he tried to suppress the low rumble that escaped him as he moaned.

"Me too," I whispered. I quickly pulled back and bounced away. I left him standing in the bedroom as I grabbed my bag and flung it over my shoulder.

My cell phone buzzed.

He's been cleared.

I couldn't help the wide, cheeky smile that formed as I read Tara's text message.

Blakely sauntered back into the living room, wearing his signature cool-and-collected look. But inside, I was sure there was a raging storm threatening to drown him.

"Let me guess. I passed the background check," he said.

I typed a message back to Tara, telling her to get his paperwork in order and that I would have him stop there soon.

"You did," I said as I finished typing my message.

He smiled, and I leaned against the counter.

"I'm offering you the job, Mr. Blakely. Do you want it?"

There was no mistaking my tone. He knew *exactly* what I was asking.

He swallowed, his Adam's apple taunting me. He didn't speak. Instead, he watched me, and in my mind, I created a million different scenarios, a million different answers to my question.

Truth was, he wanted me. I'd seen it in those few times he'd let down his guard.

But he also knew I wanted him, and I wasn't shy about it. I no longer questioned if he could handle a girl like me. Instead, I wondered if he could handle the added benefits I was offering.

After all, workplace romances were usually forbidden.

CHAPTER FOUR

My words hung heavy in the air between us as I waited for him to respond. As each second ticked by, I was beginning to think I had overreached. I was used to being aggressive, but maybe he couldn't handle a woman like me. Out of fear of being slut-shamed, many women acted like delicate creatures who didn't speak out of turn.

But that wasn't me.

I knew what I wanted, and I went for it. If that made people consider me a whore, so be it.

I could sleep in the bed I'd made.

The real question was, would Blakely be joining me?

A better question would be, did I *want* a man who couldn't handle a woman like me?

Hell no.

He exhaled slowly. "Yes, I want it." He spoke just above a whisper, so quietly I thought I might have hallucinated his admission. But the darkness in his eyes betrayed his need.

And I knew I had him right where I wanted him.

I smiled, brushing against him as I passed.

"Let's get an early dinner."

But what I really meant was, let's get home early tonight.

★ ★ ★

I slurped my Mei Fun noodles, swiveling the next bite onto my chopsticks. I had opted for a tiny Chinese restaurant down the street from my apartment. It took exactly thirteen minutes to walk there. Twenty-six minutes plus eating time was all that stood between Blakely and me alone in my apartment.

I felt the excitement from my cheeks to my core.

I had chosen a table near the windows, but Blakely quickly moved us to a back-corner booth, positioned right beside the restaurant's only back exit. A collage of photographs that depicted the streets of New York through its many decades of change lined the wall behind Blakely. I watched him scoop a bite of fried rice and kung pao chicken into his mouth as he scanned the room. His eyes never left the area behind me. I had no idea what was there, but I had an amazing imagination. It had to be something interesting. After all, he hadn't spoken to or looked at me since we'd ordered our food.

I imagined Big Foot was putting on a show. Or maybe that shark tornado that was terrorizing the East Coast. Hell, maybe the devil incarnate was right behind me, playing a game of chess with a long-haired man who eerily resembled...

"How's the food?" I asked.

He nodded.

"Not a Chinese fan?"

"I like Chinese."

What the hell was going on? Sure, our relationship had changed drastically in just a matter of minutes, but this was a little ridiculous.

I liked to be teased, but I didn't like games that played with my emotions. Blakely's mixed signals were giving me whiplash.

I exhaled dramatically. "What's so interesting?"

He glanced at me. "Nothing."

I held his gaze, daring him to be the first to back away. He blinked and scanned the room.

Son of a bitch.

James Blakely was going to be a difficult conquest, but I hadn't yet thrown in the towel.

I slurped the last bit of soda from my cup and tossed my napkin on my plate, sinking back into the plastic lining of my seat. I crossed my arms over my chest and turned, scanning the room.

I shrugged. "Seems like your typical restaurant."

I turned around and locked eyes with Blakely.

"Miss Tate—"

"Jezebel," I corrected.

"I'm here to do an important job, and I'd like to focus all of my energy on keeping you safe."

I swallowed. He was right. Keeping me safe was his job, and it was ten times harder to do in public—and without backup.

I nodded my submission, my eyes dropping to his wide, lean chest. The restaurant's air conditioning was in full force, and the vent just above Blakely's seat had his nipples peaked.

I groaned. Damn him. I could've sworn he was doing that intentionally.

"Should we hire a team?" I asked, letting my eyes trail the length of his toned arms. The stark contrast between his tanned skin and the white cotton of his shirt was oddly erotic.

Holy fuck, I needed Mr. Dependable tonight.

"Miss Tate."

I rolled my eyes. "Jez-e-bel," I said. "Seriously, Blakely. We need to work on this."

He arched an eyebrow, a crooked grin forming across his

perfectly sculpted face. "Let's make a deal."

Intrigued, I folded my arms across the tabletop and leaned toward him, smiling. "I'm listening."

"I'll stop calling you Miss Tate—"

"And ma'am," I cut in.

He grinned. "I'll stop calling you Miss Tate *and* ma'am if you stop giving me those come-fuck-me eyes."

I gasped, and I was sure my jaw slapped the floor before I yanked it shut. A wicked grin crossed my face, and I bit my lower lip.

"Deal," I said as I crossed my toes.

Hell, even Cinderella herself would've lied.

★ ★ ★

"Will you be staying in for the rest of the night?" Blakely asked as we filed into my apartment. He closed the door behind us as I tossed my bag onto the kitchen counter.

"I was hoping we could," I replied. "Did you have other plans?"

"I'd like to get my things." He pulled his cell phone from his back pocket and pressed a button. The screen lit up. "I should be back within an hour. Stay inside. Lock the door."

"I like it when you order me around," I purred.

He grasped the doorknob, yanked it open, and turned on his heel. "Good. Do as you're told." There was a devilish hint in his eyes, and I couldn't help but play along.

I bounced toward him, leaning against the doorframe. Only inches separated us, but within those inches, the air changed. The static charge between us was evident, and the darkness in his usually bright, sapphire-blue eyes told me he felt it, too.

Christ, this man was going to be the best fuck of my life.

I couldn't wait to let go of what little reservations I had around him and let him take me all the way.

In truth, I hadn't had a good fuck...ever. Mr. Dependable was fantastic, don't get me wrong, but my exes had no idea how to work a woman's body—or a man's, for that matter. They were no different than angsty, horny teens in a losing game.

But James Blakely reeked of a sex god.

He knew it. I knew it. Hell, anyone who looked at him knew it.

From his lean, muscular frame to his commanding eyes, he took control.

And a small part of me was willing to let go and give it to him.

I'd hardly consider myself submissive, but the thought of releasing control to Blakely made my toes curl.

He could tie me up and spank me *any* damn day.

I angled my head back to meet his eyes. A small smile formed, but he quickly brushed it away. I dragged my teeth against the skin of my lower lip and relished the sight of his eyes following that movement.

"Yes, sir," I said.

The look that flashed across his face nearly brought me to my knees. There was power there, a strength I was sure he rarely delved into. A dominant man to his core, Blakely desperately needed to let loose.

And it sure as hell was going to be with me.

He closed the door, and I stood on my tiptoes to watch him through the peephole. His hand hadn't yet left the doorknob when the other ran through his tussled brown hair. Soon, I'd be running my hands through it, too. He let out a long breath and then turned to face the door. He stared at the peephole, and even though the rational part of me told me there was no way he could see me, I convinced myself he could. He was staring straight back at me, taunting me, daring me to make the first move.

Had his control faltered?

I definitely didn't want to sit around, asking myself what-ifs.

I grasped the doorknob and began turning the handle, but before I could get the door open, he turned and walked away.

I groaned, locked the door, and stalked down the hallway.

This game of cat and mouse was getting old.

CHAPTER FIVE

I walked to the bathroom and yanked off my clothes, leaving them in a pile on the floor. After stepping into the shower, I let the water cascade down my frame and watched it swirl down the drain. It felt like an hour had passed before I finally decided to wash my hair.

I finished my routine and stepped out of the glass enclosure, wrapping a towel around myself. I ran my fingers through my dripping hair and jumped when a loud knock erupted through my silent, empty apartment.

I tiptoed into the living room, leaving a trail of water in my wake.

"It's me," a voice said.

I unlocked the door and opened it to let him inside—bags and all.

He took a step forward and came to a screeching halt. The sharp inhalation he took had no chance of escaping as his widened eyes trailed the length of my body. One hand on the doorknob, I used the other to hold the bunched towel at my breasts. I silently thanked God that I'd chosen one of the smaller towels to wrap myself in. I didn't have to look down to know he was getting a good show. The hem of the towel rested against my upper thighs, only inches below my aching core. I hadn't dried my hair, and I could feel the water droplets slide down my curves.

He licked his lips, and I knew I had him right where I wanted him.

I turned on my heel and sauntered down the hallway. "Remember to lock up," I said over my shoulder.

I heard the door close, and just as I reached my bedroom door, I dropped the towel, giving him full view of one of my greatest assets. I turned toward my closet, stealing a peek down the hall, and he was exactly where I'd left him.

We locked eyes until I disappeared into my closet, grinning.

I listened for footsteps but heard none. I dressed quickly, opting for only a loose, thigh-length nightgown, and returned to the bathroom. I towel-dried my hair, finger-brushed it, and cleaned up my mess before joining Blakely in the living room. He hadn't moved from the doorway, and I chuckled as I passed him.

"You can come in, y'know," I said. "This is your place, too."

"This isn't going to work," he said.

I stopped and spun around. "Why?"

He dropped his bags and stalked toward me, closing the space between us. He pushed me past the bar stools.

The counter jabbed into my flesh, and I gasped. I lost control of myself and reached behind his neck, running my fingers through his silky strands and tugging his lips down to meet mine. I found the hem of his shirt with my other hand and reached underneath, scratching my nails against each defined ridge of his torso.

He leaned down and brushed his lips against mine.

If anyone could orgasm from a kiss, it would be from this one—I knew this to be true. I arched into him as his hands wrapped around my body and grabbed my ass. I gasped into his mouth, drunk on his scent.

"This is why," he said breathlessly.

And then he pulled away.

I grabbed the bar stools to balance my weight and fought to control my breathing.

"What the fuck?" I shouted. "I like to play games, Blakely, don't get me wrong. I can be a tease and I can be teased, but I need to know I'll get the prize at some point."

"That's not going to happen," he said calmly. "*This*"—he motioned between us—"can't happen."

"Why the hell not?" I asked, finding the strength to step forward. With every step I took, he took two more back. Groaning, I stopped and crossed my arms over my chest, knowing perfectly well my breasts would perk up and pop out against the thin fabric of my nightgown. "And don't you dare say you don't want it, because it's obvious that you do."

I glanced down, my eyes lingering on his impressive erection.

"Jezebel, you're paying me to protect you."

Thank God he got my name right this time.

"Yeah, so? I don't need your protection in bed," I argued.

"I can't protect you if I'm fucking you."

"I don't see the problem here."

"I won't be thinking clearly. I need to think with my brain, not my dick. I need to focus on your surroundings. I need to think critically, not emotionally."

He stepped forward. His gaze dropped, his eyes darkening. The lust I saw there screamed back at me. With just the look in his eyes, he threatened to take me here, now, and even though that was everything I wanted, I still backed away until he had me pinned against a wall in the hallway. He caged me between his arms, the scruff of his chin brushing against my cheek. My palms were flat against the wall behind me, its coolness almost painful against my skin. Every fiber of my being was on fire.

I desperately needed him to touch me.

I didn't want James Blakely to be gentle.

I didn't need him to love me.

I needed him to fuck me. Hard.

It took everything I had to strengthen my wobbly knees.

I was getting desperate. It had been too long since I'd trusted someone with my body. It had been too long since I'd wanted someone to trust me with theirs.

"And when I'm around you," he said, his breath hot on my cheek, "the only thing I can think about is fucking you until your eyes roll back, your limbs stop working, and you can't remember your own name."

He leaned closer and brushed his lips against my ear.

A shiver shot through me, and I scratched my nails against the wall behind me. My eyes rolled closed as several images flashed in my mind.

Briefly, I fantasized about him ripping off my clothes as I worked his pants down. In an instant, he'd have me in his arms, shoving inside me. I'd cry out, the first of many screams. I'd yank his shirt over his head, relishing in the feeling of skin-on-skin contact—something I so desperately needed right now. He'd pound into me, a merciless style of fucking I'd never experienced before.

I opened my eyes to find him watching me.

Holy fuck, this man would be the death of me.

And I was perfectly okay with that.

We turned toward each other in unison, and I watched as his eyes narrowed, focusing solely on the small space between his lips and mine.

"I might surprise you. We can make this work."

I pushed off the wall and leaned against his frame. The hem of his shirt bunched beneath my fingers as I pulled him closer. He gasped, and it was by far the sexiest noise to have ever escaped a man's mouth. If I went deaf in this very moment, I'd be okay with that sound being the last thing I ever heard.

"Relationships like this never work." He breathed against my lips. "Dating your boss *never* works."

"I'm not asking you to marry me, Blakely. I'm just asking you to fuck me until my legs buckle and I beg you to take me just a little bit harder."

His eyes widened as he dragged his teeth against his lower lip. He was hard. His length pressed against my stomach, digging into my skin.

He may not have approved of office romances...

But he didn't pull away. He let my hands linger as I explored his body through the fabric of his shirt. I slipped my hands beneath it and slowly worked my way up his chest. I reached around, sliding my fingers across the smooth skin of his taut back. I teased the length of his spine.

I stood on my tiptoes and grazed his lips.

"And if I kiss you now?" I asked. "Would you push me away? Would you stop me? Or could you *take* what you *want*?"

He didn't answer, and I was sure that was because he didn't know. He wouldn't know until I made the move.

So I did.

I dug my fingers into the flesh of his back while I leaned forward, pressing my mouth against his.

He groaned when our lips met. But he caved. His tongue was eagerly searching my mouth. He craved the taste of me just as much as I craved the taste of him.

Hot damn, this man was an amazing kisser. He kissed and licked and stroked and nipped at all the right moments.

He grabbed my hands that rested at his waist and brought them behind his neck. His fingers lightly caressed the skin of my arms as he worked his way down the length of my body. When he found the hem of my nightgown, he cupped my ass and lifted me. Instinctively, I wrapped my legs around his waist and gasped into his mouth as he rubbed his erection against my quivering core.

He pulled back and watched me as he ground against my clit. I scratched my fingernails against his scalp, tugging the strands of his hair.

"Fuck..." I breathed. "So good."

"Tell me what you want," he said. His voice was deep, dark, demanding.

My three favorite things.

"Oh, God, don't stop. Don't stop touching me," I begged. "Just one night..."

I was breathless, needy. I'd even submit to him tonight if I had to.

I was moving close to the edge, so close to my release. He kissed me quick, fast, hard, and then pulled back. His mouth latched on to my nipple, soaking the fabric of my nightgown. I cried out when he grazed his teeth against the sensitive nub.

"Fuck!"

I was close, so close.

And then everything stopped.

A hard banging against my door vibrated the wall he supported me against. The orgasmic wave blew away, and reality kicked in. In a swift motion, Blakely moved from the wall and sprinted toward my bedroom. He dropped me onto my bed.

"Stay here," he ordered.

Shocked at the abrupt change, I stayed there, my nightgown hiked up and my legs spread open.

But ever the gentleman, Blakely's eyes never left mine.

I nodded in response.

He stepped backward, reached behind his back, and pulled out a gun.

I gasped. "Where the hell've you been hiding that thing?"

Feeling suddenly vulnerable, I tugged my nightgown down and stood. He did a quick hand maneuver that made the gun click before turning on his heel and stalking down the hallway toward the door.

There was another set of knocks, this time louder and more frequent.

Whoever was at my door wanted inside—badly.

But since when did burglars knock?

Since when did burglars get past the locked door to my building?

I tiptoed toward my bedroom door and watched as Blakely reached the front door. He glanced back and mouthed that I should stay.

Was he being slightly overdramatic?

Or could there be real danger outside my door?

The optimist in me took over, and I shrugged off the concern. What was the chance that someone would break in and make all this noise before the sun had even set?

I walked down the hallway, and as I reached him, he faced me. He sighed, his eyes narrowing.

"I told you to stay there," he whispered.

"It could be anyone," I responded, speaking just as quietly.

"I'm only worried about *one* person," he said.

I blinked, swallowing the knot in my throat. He was right. I was being foolish. I'd hired him to protect me, and that was what he was trying to do. But before I could run back to the bedroom and hide under the covers like an eight-year-old, the lock on my door unlatched.

I blinked once. Twice.

Another latch released.

My heart was pounding in my ears so loudly I hadn't heard Blakely speak until he grabbed my arm in a tight squeeze. I swallowed down my nausea and met his eyes.

"Who else has a key?" he repeated quietly.

I couldn't think. I couldn't breathe. Had I given anyone else a key?

No. I hadn't even trusted a maid to clean my apartment. I barely trusted my accountant.

I shook my head.

The doorknob twisted, the door opened, and the intruder took a step inside.

In a flash, Blakely grabbed the doorknob, yanked the door toward him, and then thrust it forward again. He made contact, and the intruder cried out, falling to the floor in a loud thump. Blakely rounded the door, pointed the pistol, and—

"Shit," he said, lowering his weapon. I watched as he lifted the back of his shirt, revealing a hidden holster. He sheathed the weapon and helped the intruder to his feet.

Confused, I yanked the door open so quickly it smashed into the wall.

Blakely helped Tara inside. Her face was stained crimson as she held her nose. The front of her shirt was splattered with blood.

"Oh my God!" I said, running to the bathroom to grab

my first-aid kit. I returned to find her sitting on my couch, desperately trying to avoid making a bloody mess.

I dropped the kit, and it broke open, scattering supplies everywhere.

"Shit!" I said, sinking to my knees to grab the gauze.

I handed her a bunch, and we sat in an awkward silence until the bleeding stopped. When it finally did, she cleaned herself up with antibacterial liquid and let Blakely inspect the damage.

"Doesn't seem to be broken," he said.

"Well, that's good, right?" I asked, smiling.

Tara nodded and dried her tears.

"I'm sorry, Tara," I said.

"I'm not," Blakely said.

Tara looked away, but I didn't. I met his glare.

"I'm sorry you got hurt, yes, but this is what you pay me to do. Coming in like that, especially without announcing yourself, was the worst thing you could've done."

I groaned. "Could you be a bigger dick right now?"

He opened his mouth to speak, but something stopped him before he made that mistake. It could have been the death daggers I was throwing at him with my eyes.

"Tara," I said, softening my voice. "I'm so sorry. I completely forgot I'd given you a key."

She smiled. "It's okay. He's right. I shouldn't have just let myself in."

I shrugged. "It's never been an issue before."

"It is now. Key, please," Blakely said, offering her his hand.

It took everything I had not to reach forward and smack him.

Yes, he was my bodyguard.

Yes, he was just doing his job.

But did he have to be a dick while doing it?

Before I could respond, Tara did. "Why can't I keep it?"

"Because next time, I'll shoot the intruder. You're lucky Jezebel didn't listen and distracted me." He tore his gaze from Tara's to meet mine. "But that won't happen again, either."

And in an instant, the anger I felt dissipated. He was direct, commanding, dominant. And I felt his words travel through my ears and resonate with my throbbing core.

I was sure I was doing it again, but I didn't care. I'd give him my come-fuck-me eyes every damn time he tried to boss me around.

Because it was sexy as hell.

He cleared his throat. "Still, you're very lucky. If she hadn't disobeyed me..."

Had anyone ever sounded this sexy before? I mean, my best friend had a bandaged nose, puffy, red eyes, and the sniffles, yet all I could think about was Blakely's voice when he said I *disobeyed* him.

And I was dying to see just how naughty I could be.

She nodded, sniffling, and handed him her key. He slid it into his pocket.

"I, uh...I came for a reason. I got worried when you didn't answer your phone and then the door."

"Oh, right." I was busy nearly fucking my bodyguard. "I was—"

Blakely cleared his throat but didn't look at me.

"I was busy. Sorry."

She shook her head. "It's okay. Better we talk in person."

"About?"

"We got a letter," she said, pulling a crisp white envelope from her bag.

My world came crashing down. Everything slowed, from the way she reached forward to hand me the letter to the movement of her mouth when she spoke something I couldn't understand. Time seemed to stand still as she offered it to me. A knot formed in my throat, threatening to choke me, and my vision blurred.

I hadn't received a letter in weeks. I was beginning to think he'd forgotten about me. After all, I'd made discovering my location difficult. I used a pen name, I never spoke of my residence, and the only way to contact me was through my agent. I didn't use social media. I didn't have an email address where readers could reach me.

I'd strengthened the wall between me and the rest of the world so much that I'd convinced myself I was safe. That this threat wasn't real. I'd believed I was only hiring a bodyguard because of Tara's overprotective tendencies—not because of some masked maniac.

But he was back. He'd found me.

I didn't need to open it to know it was from him.

Tara remained with her arm outstretched, waiting for me to take the letter from her.

But I couldn't. I couldn't move, couldn't think, couldn't breathe.

I could feel his hands wrap around my neck and grip, squeezing just enough so I knew he was there, watching me, waiting for a weakness.

He never fully took my life from me, but he played with it.

Sometimes, he'd give me just enough freedom to make me believe he was gone, that this wasn't really happening.

Other times, he'd be so close I was sure he brushed past me on the street.

But this time, I didn't have to take the letter. I didn't have to be the one who opened it. I didn't have to read his words alone.

The night after I received his first letter, I barricaded myself in my room and slept on the floor beneath my bed. The next day, I realized how stupid that was. Underneath the bed was the first place people checked. The next night, I slept in my bathtub. I didn't leave my apartment for a month.

I wrote my second novel in that month, because writing and crying was all I could do. That was all he'd let me do.

Eventually, I'd convinced myself that I was overreacting. And that was our routine. I'd get a letter, freak out, and then forget about it.

Blakely grabbed the letter from her and ripped it open. Pictures from today spilled onto his lap.

There were pictures of me leaving Tara's office and shopping at the stores down the block from my apartment.

There were pictures of Blakely and me on the street, in an intimate embrace. Our faces were only inches apart, nearly kissing. Blakely's face was scratched out, unrecognizable. Written above us, in bold, red letters that dripped as if the ink hadn't dried before being shoved in the envelope, was the answer to the one question I'd been too afraid to ask, as if he were already in my head.

He can't stop me.

I gasped when Blakely shifted and the pictures slid to the side, showcasing the final image on display. Tears burned in my eyes and spilled down my cheeks.

It was a picture of me in my apartment. I was sitting at the kitchen counter, looking at my phone. A water bottle was beside me.

I glanced at the window. Sunlight flooded in, cascading my apartment in beautiful white rays. The irony stung. My legs burned even though I hadn't moved. I ache to run over, throw open my curtains, and find the apartment he used to stalk me, to invade my privacy.

He'd found me.

After months of letters, he'd never found my home.

Not until today. Not until I was reckless. Not until my desperate desire to fuck Blakely consumed my thoughts.

Today was the first time I truly hadn't feared the man who stalked me. In fact, I'd barely thought of him, and he knew it.

So, he took that safety away.

"These were all taken today," I whispered.

Blakely collected the photos and opened the envelope to drop them inside.

"Wait," I said, grabbing the photos from his hands.

I fell to my knees in front of my coffee table and laid them down. The backs were blank—all but one. The photo of me sitting alone in my apartment had a sloppy handwritten message across the back. Like the other message, the red ink dripped, smearing across the white canvas. Leaving the pictures on the table, I pushed myself to my feet and wrapped my arms around my chest.

I reread his message to me a dozen times over.

Soon.

CHAPTER SIX

Blakely gathered the stack of photos into a bunch and retreated down the hall into his bedroom. I didn't know what he was going to do with them, and I didn't care. I couldn't focus on anything except the all-consuming sense of dread that washed over me.

I'd never felt so alone.

I stood in an apartment with two people who would do anything for me, yet I was completely alone.

They didn't understand what I was feeling. Sure, they sympathized with me. But they didn't have a stalker. They didn't have someone watching them during their most private moments.

I gasped.

Oh God.

Had he seen the show I'd put on for Blakely earlier?

Bile worked its way into my mouth, and I ran down the hall, tripping over my feet as I lunged into the bathroom. I heaved into the toilet. Tears burned my eyes, and I let them fall. I leaned against the toilet seat, resting my forehead against my arm, and let it all out.

When the sobs slowed and my senses returned, I realized someone was rubbing my back. I pushed myself off the seat to find Blakely holding back my hair. I searched his eyes and found they mirrored my pain. They ached for me, pleaded with me. The worry, the anger, the dread... It was all too much. His emotions were too much.

I hated my life.

And in that moment, I was sure my eyes betrayed that.

I'd told Tara once. I'd told her I never wanted this. I wanted to be a writer. I wanted to be invisible.

Writers weren't supposed to be famous. Not like this, anyway.

She told me I sounded unappreciative.

And she was right.

She told me never to speak like that again.

So I never did.

But looking at the emotions swarming in Blakely's eyes, I felt that anger again.

The pity staring back at me was suffocating.

I couldn't look at him anymore, so I stood, wiping the vomit from my lips on the back of my hand. He stood with me, releasing my hair but letting his hands linger. He lightly brushed the skin of my arms. My skin prickled with each stroke, electric shocks surging through me and sending waves of frustration straight to my heart.

I pulled away from him. "Stop. Just stop! I don't need your pity."

I walked backward, desperate to escape the enclosed space, but he sidestepped, locking me in.

"I don't pity you, Jezebel," he said quietly.

"Stop it! Just...get out of my way," I said, trying to bypass him.

"You're going to be okay. I promise I will keep you safe."

His words washed over me, but instead of bringing peace, they brought pain. I couldn't listen. I couldn't think about this. I just needed to get away. I needed to be alone, to escape.

My eyes felt dry, even though I was sure they were anything but. My head was pounding, and my heart felt like I'd tossed it up with my Chinese. I couldn't deal with this. I couldn't handle this again.

I was a writer who desperately tried to experience as little as possible.

I didn't want to live through my characters. I didn't want to know the world.

I just wanted to live alone, in peace. I just wanted to forget everything.

The loss, the pain, the anger, the fear...

At Tara's request, I'd written my first book to cope with my role in my parents' deaths. I'd written to escape the thoughts that haunted me day in, day out. Those words, which I'd unknowingly prayed would bring me reprieve, had brought me to him. This life was my hell, a place I'd penned just for my personal damnation.

But I didn't fear for my soul. I knew I'd lost it the day my parents died.

I just wanted to stop being afraid.

Afraid of him.

Afraid of the street when the light goes out while I'm walking.

Afraid of the not-too-distant car alarm that suddenly blares.

Afraid of the barking dog who's quickly silenced.

I wanted to stop being reminded that he was out there, somewhere, watching me. I wanted to live my days in seclusion, counting the moments until I was forced to account for the sins of my past.

I curled my fingers, scratching at my palms, and brought

my fists down upon Blakely's chest.

"Leave me alone!" I yelled. "Just go away!"

I screamed as I poured everything I had into my arms. In a mesmerizing rhythm, my fists smashed against his chest repeatedly, but he never flinched. He never moved. He simply blocked the door and let me fight off my invisible attacker.

I didn't stop until I could no longer feel my hands or cry or scream.

I hiccupped through each breath as I fought to control the storm of emotions raging within me.

My legs buckled and I collapsed, but he grabbed me before I hit the tile. He sank to the floor beside me, grabbed on to my frail frame, and cradled me in his arms. We sat there, unmoving, until I could finally see, breathe, think.

He held me until the light from the sun faded and darkness filled my empty apartment.

CHAPTER SEVEN

I woke in bed, alone. The birds were chirping, and the sun was annoyingly bright. I rubbed the sleep from my eyes, wincing. I'd spent most of the night crying.

And Blakely had never left my side.

My gaze flickered to the pillow beside mine. He wasn't there now, but I knew he had been all night. With my fingers, I traced the indent he'd made in the still-warm sheets.

I sat up and strolled into the bathroom, leisurely brushing my teeth and washing my face.

I wasn't in a hurry to face him.

I wasn't in a hurry to face reality.

I stripped out of my clothes and stood, unmoving, in the shower, letting the water cascade over me. I counted to one hundred at least ten times before I finally washed, rinsed, and dressed. When I strolled into the kitchen, I found Blakely sitting at the breakfast bar, drinking coffee.

"Good morning," he said, setting down his mug.

"Morning."

"Are you hungry? I was thinking about making eggs and bacon."

He stood and walked around the counter and into the kitchen.

I shook my head, opened the refrigerator door, and grabbed a bottle of water. I took three swigs before the imagery hit me. I was doing this same thing when he photographed me yesterday. Feeling sick, I tossed the bottle into the sink and leaned against the counter. I closed my eyes and counted to three, taking long, slow breaths.

My mother had sworn by this stress-relieving technique, but it never worked for me. At least, not after her death. The idea mocked me, though, as I still tried it.

My heart ached. I wished I could call her. I wished I could run to her and never look back. But the accident that took her life left me with nothing but overwhelming guilt.

I opened my eyes to find Blakely watching me. He offered a small smile before reaching into his back pocket and pulling out an envelope. He didn't speak when he handed it to me.

I swallowed down the lump in my throat. "You're leaving," I said, eyes on the envelope but hands at my sides.

"I— What?"

"Don't sugarcoat it. I wouldn't want to stay either." I looked past his dark frame. "Just give that to Tara. She'll take care of everything."

It was then I realized two things.

First, Tara wasn't here. She must have left sometime after my bathroom meltdown. I hoped Blakely had seen her home safely, but I knew that wasn't the case. After all, he was my bodyguard, not hers. I knew he wouldn't leave my side.

Second, all the curtains in my living room had been drawn shut.

"You closed them," I said.

Blakely followed my gaze and nodded. "It's best for now."

I exhaled sharply. "Yeah, I guess." Especially if I had to watch my own back now.

I walked into the living room, leaving Blakely and his resignation letter in the kitchen.

"Miss Tate," he said, following close behind me.

I chuckled. "So, we're back to Miss Tate? I was ready to fuck you yesterday, and then I practically—" I gasped, spinning around. "Are you okay?" I closed the space between us, reaching for his shirt. I grabbed the hem and yanked it up.

Stunned, Blakely fumbled backward, dropping the envelope and grabbing on to my hands. He pushed me away and quickly covered himself. I searched his eyes.

Unlike last night, they were unreadable.

"I'm fine," he said.

I shook my head and threw my arms around his neck, pulling him into a tight embrace. I rested against the curve of his neck and closed my eyes, taking him in with each deep inhalation.

"I'm so sorry," I whispered. "I'm so, so sorry."

I was shaking. I couldn't believe I'd intentionally physically injured the one person who had sworn to remain by my side through the darkest of times.

"Jezebel, I want you to forget about it."

I pulled back so I could see his face, but I left my arms wrapped around his neck, and he left his hands resting against the small of my back. I felt safe in his arms, which only made his leaving that much harder.

"Is this why you're resigning? I promise— I swear it'll never happen again."

"Yes, it will—"

"No! I promise. Please don't leave. Not now. Not at the worst possible time to be leaving," I begged.

"Why do you think I'm leaving?" he asked.

"The letter. You're resigning."

He furrowed his brow.

"You're not? You're not quitting?"

He shook his head, and relief flooded me. In a world where I could trust only myself, it was nice to know he was on my side.

"Inside the envelope is a list of requirements. That's all."

This time, I arched an eyebrow, but I also took a step back. "Requirements?"

He nodded. "There are some things I need to do my job."

"Oh, yes, of course. Whatever you need."

"Some are basic things that are discussed in the package you gave me—a phone, a computer, a car. But there are some other things we should consider."

I nodded. "Okay. Sure."

"We need a surveillance system, and you'll be getting an alarm. Why you don't already have one is beyond me."

"I added another lock."

"I see that," he said, glancing at my front door. "We also need to talk about adding to your security detail. You really should consider adding anywhere from one to three more men."

"A four-person security detail?" I asked. "Isn't that a bit much?"

He shrugged. "It could be, but in the end, you'll be four times more likely to survive."

The room fell silent.

"I— That's not what I meant. I just mean, it's easier for me to do my job when I have a team. That's all."

I nodded. "I'll think about it."

"Also, we need to leave Manhattan."

I didn't speak as I considered his request. I'd feared it'd come to this, but I was stubborn. I didn't want to give up the final string that tied me to my old life, a life when I only hid from my past indiscretions.

I shook my head. "I'm not ready yet."

"Jezebel, you really need to—"

"You think I haven't considered this? It's all I think about! But the last thing I need is for him to run me from my home, too. I won't do it. Not unless there's absolutely no other choice." I crossed my arms over my chest. I'd cave on just about anything else—anything but that.

"When the time comes, you won't fight me on this?" he asked.

"Don't you mean *if the time comes*?" I asked.

He didn't need to respond. We both knew the truth, and there was no need to speak it.

CHAPTER EIGHT

In the back of the taxi, I watched buildings blur by. Blakely had just made a call to some distant connection to confirm that my neighbors weren't serial killers. He'd had them checked out and determined they were safe within minutes. I was happy, but that meant my *real* stalker was still out there.

And we weren't any closer to discovering his identity.

We stopped at a light, and I locked eyes with the driver in the car beside us. Quickly, he looked away.

Could that be him?

Could he see me now?

Was he following us?

I turned away from the window and faced Blakely, who sat beside me. He was scribbling notes in a small notebook he kept in his back pocket. The cover was creased where he'd sat on it too many times. Its black color had long since faded to a dark gray.

"Which store are we going to?" I asked.

"A home-improvement store. I think I can get most everything on my list there."

"Tara is already working on getting you a phone and computer," I said, remembering my earlier promises.

He nodded. "Good. What about a car? We'll need special additions, like tinted windows, airless tires, bulletproof siding."

"Tara can help with that, too," I said quietly.

I exhaled slowly, trying not to think about the dangers

that lurked around every corner when I wasn't hidden safely behind my apartment door.

In a matter of minutes, my stalker had elevated his game, bringing my happy-go-lucky world to a screeching halt. I'd been careless—stupid, even—and I was mentally preparing myself for what the coming days would bring. I couldn't venture out alone anymore—such reckless behavior would undoubtedly be my end.

We reached the home-improvement store sooner than I anticipated. Blakely paid the driver, and we walked inside.

Feeling nervous, I walked close by Blakely's side. Only when our arms touched did I feel I was safe enough to explore. I scanned my surroundings as Blakely tossed items into the basket I carried.

The store was full of shoppers—mostly couples who seemed to be embarking on a do-it-yourself home project. I smiled at a woman who seemed less than thrilled to watch the man she was with assess tools. He stared at two hammers as if there was a difference between them. I wasn't convinced there was.

When I'd bought my apartment, I'd hated the floor plan, so I'd bulldozed through it and started from scratch. That part had been awful. I'd spent hours in a store like this one, but when the revamp was completed and I could finally decorate the rooms, I'd known I had made the right decision. Eventually, this stranger would feel that way, too.

"Can I help you find something?" someone asked.

I jolted behind Blakely, my heart beating in overdrive. I was sure I looked on edge. Adrenaline coursed through my veins, a feeling eerily like a situation I'd only recently written about in my latest novel. I realized I hadn't given the scene the justice it deserved.

Blakely cleared his throat as he extended an arm toward me. "*Umm*, no, thanks. We're fine. We're just picking up a home-security system."

The kid speaking looked no older than seventeen. His eyes were bright, vibrant, as if he had no familiarity with the dangers in this world. A sloppy mess of red curls cropped his head, and it wobbled every time he spoke. It looked like a wig that would soon topple over. "You came to the right place. We have some fantastic options. How secure are you looking to go?"

"Pretty secure," Blakely said.

Pointing to a shelved box, the kid said, "I'd go with our all-in-one camera system. You can hook up this bad boy, and then once you download the free app to any smart device—like a cell phone or tablet—you can watch a live feed of your house from anywhere you have Wi-Fi access. It comes with four cameras, but you can buy extra. And the cameras can be used outdoors, too. Don't worry about the elements." He offered a shining smile.

Blakely nodded and grabbed the box from the shelf, reading the back. "Does it come with an actual alarm system?"

"Sure does. It'll work through a phone line, so the police and fire department will be notified if it goes off. They'll call you to make sure everything is okay."

"Why do we even need all this? You'll be there," I asked.

"The alarm system and cameras are more of a deterrent," Blakely answered. "People are less likely to do something stupid when they're on camera or if the police will be notified if they break down the door."

"Right..." the kid said, chuckling. "We don't exactly

market it that way, but I guess that's true. Keep in mind that it's a completely dependable system. It's not just there for looks."

The kid winked at me, and I rolled my eyes.

"We'll take it," Blakely said, ignoring the kid's pointed comment.

Within the hour, we were back in my neighborhood, but once we reached my apartment and ditched our bags, my phone beeped.

I glanced at the screen, which displayed a text from Tara. "Let's go by Tara's office," I said. "She has your phone and laptop."

I wrote her back.

Be there soon.

The taxi ride was shorter than usual, and we were at Tara's office building before she had even replied to my message.

I offered a friendly hello to Tara's assistant before opening the door to Tara's office. Immediately, I was pulled into a tight embrace.

"How're you doing?" she asked.

"Struggling to breathe. You?" I joked.

Tara had a way of making me feel instantly at ease. I'd only felt such a feeling with one other person. Blakely. Tara liked numbers and order, but I relied on my gut instincts. If my emotions told me I could trust someone, I knew it to be true. Within seconds of meeting someone, I could tell if I'd connect with him or her. I'd felt it with Tara, with Blakely, and so far, this superpower of mine hadn't let me down.

Now, as I stood in Tara's office, I felt the pain of the world slowly wash away. I wasn't a stalked writer. I was just a girl in the office my friend often fell asleep in after working long hours.

Giving me a sharp glare, Tara released me but didn't back away. I knew she was waiting for a more honest answer. After years of friendship, I could read her like a book.

I sighed. "Been better, but I'm dealing."

"Don't let her shut down, Mr. Blakely," she scolded, crossing her arms over her chest.

I rolled my eyes. "I'm not a child, Tara, and by the way, *nice* digs," I said, holding her at arm's length so I could take in her outfit. I desperately needed a subject change, and Tara's latest purchase would make for a perfect distraction.

"You like?" she asked, reaching down and pulling on the hem of her bright-red cocktail dress.

"I *love*," I said. "I wish I could pull off the colors you can. I'd wear this in a second."

Tara's skin was dark, so bright colors worked to her advantage. She looked stunningly flawless in every crazy color she'd ever worn.

I could never hide my jealousy well.

"Is this for me?" Blakely asked, breaking my trance. Apparently Blakely didn't get the subject-change notice.

Tara faced him and nodded. "Yes. Both are brand-new, and they're insured. Let me know if you need to file a claim for any reason."

"Did you charge these to my account?" I asked.

She nodded. Tara wasn't just my literary agent; she was also my best friend who occasionally did work an assistant would do. I'd tried to pop the bubble I'd surrounded myself with long enough to hire an assistant, but I couldn't do it. I couldn't trust someone the way I trusted her, so I'd given Tara a credit card for times when she needed to spend money on me that wasn't included in the literary agent category.

"I've also ordered another card with Mr. Blakely's name on it, but it'll take a couple weeks to get here."

I nodded. "He can use mine in the meantime," I said.

"I wanted to talk to you about a car," Blakely added, his eyes on Tara.

While Tara and Blakely talked the pros and cons of cars over SUVs and whether the additional expense of bulletproof siding was necessary, I helped myself to some coffee. The aroma of coffee beans wafted through the air, and briefly, I closed my eyes, letting my senses soak up the sensation. I'd always been a coffee person. I inherited the love for coffee from my mom, who couldn't go a day without several cups. I added a splash of cream and a few scoops of sugar before walking to the wall of windows that separated Tara's office from the rest of the world.

I stared at the skyline, letting its beauty sink in and distract me from eavesdropping. I had no interest in discussing the car detailing.

There was nothing my love affair with Manhattan couldn't cure. All I needed to do was stare at the cityscape, take in the smells, and I was hooked. I was a different person when I was in Manhattan. Back home, I was a social butterfly, but here, in Manhattan, I was a functional shut-in. And I was okay with that. People came from all over the world to start over in this city.

No one understood me the way Manhattan did.

No one would *ever* understand me the way Manhattan could.

CHAPTER NINE

I stared at the screen of my cell phone, scrolling through the email message I'd just received. The weight I'd been carrying on my shoulders seemed to lift as I read each word, my excitement building. Looking up, I smiled at Blakely, who was kneeling beside the front door, setting up the new security system we'd just gotten.

"We'll need a six-digit code," he said. His eyes met mine.

"How about 1-2-3-4-5-6," I said.

"Really?" he asked, not amused.

"Think about it. That's the last code a person would use, so it's the last code an intruder would enter. It's like making your email password *password*."

"Another code, Jezebel."

I groaned. "You pick, and I'll memorize, boss."

I watched as he punched in a security code, scribbling the number onto a sticky note before handing it to me. "Memorize this."

I saluted him, mouthed *Yes, sir*, and continued reading the email I'd received.

He shook his head at my military salute but couldn't keep the grin off his face.

"I have news," I said, letting the excitement trickle in.

"What?"

"A few months ago, my alma mater asked if I'd attend the next residency as a visiting lecturer. Appearances are part of my job, so Tara told them I'd do it."

Standing, he wiped his hands on his jeans. "When?"

"The residency begins on Monday." I flashed him a cheeky grin.

He exhaled slowly. "Monday? And you're just telling me now?" He wiped the sweat from his forehead with the back of his hand.

"Honestly, I forgot. Tara usually handles this stuff. She just tells me where to be." I shrugged.

"Shouldn't this have been mentioned as soon as you hired me?"

I sighed. "She's been a little busy lately, Blakely. Cut her some slack."

"I'm not sure it's the best idea. That doesn't give us much time to prepare."

I rolled my eyes. "Add a few days, and that's almost a week. Plenty of time!"

He frowned. "Does this really sound like an idea I'd go for?"

"Well, no... But I already agreed. I *must* do this. This isn't a signing for some bookstore I've never been to. This is my alma mater. I have friends there. A last-minute cancellation isn't going to work."

"Where?"

"Maine."

He didn't speak as he considered my request, but I could see the unease in his eyes.

"It's close. Only six or seven hours away, depending on traffic. We can drive." I smiled.

"I don't know, Jezebel..."

"We can get a suite at the same hotel where they host

the panels and readings. We'll never even have to leave the building. We'll share a room or get adjoining rooms."

He ran a hand through his hair, tussling his chocolate-brown locks. He still wasn't convinced, but I could tell I almost had him. I just needed to give him the one thing he craved. Complete control.

"I'll do whatever you ask."

His eyes met mine. "Whatever I ask whenever I ask?"

I nodded enthusiastically. "You have my word."

With a quick exhale, he agreed. "We should have Tara email over some of the bodyguard applications."

I arched an eyebrow in question.

"If we're going to do this, you need at least one more guard."

"It'll be a little ridiculous, not to mention narcissistic, if I show up with a crew of bodyguards."

"Not if the situation is considered."

"No one there knows the situation. The news about my stalker hasn't yet leaked. Tara has worked her ass off to keep this part of my career hidden from the press, from readers. No one knows, but as soon as I show up with an entourage, they'll know something is up. Or worse, they'll think I've succumbed to celebrity."

I shuddered at the thought. I'd worked hard to maintain normalcy even after my bank account reached eight figures.

The room fell silent as Blakely considered my situation. "Fine. For now, it'll be just the two of us, but remember your promises. If this gets worse, we hire more and we leave Manhattan."

"Do you know how sexy you are when you give me orders?" I asked, wiggling my brows.

"Do you know how difficult you make my job when you give me your come-fuck-me eyes?" he countered.

Smiling, I walked over and plopped onto the couch. I gently patted the open cushion, drawing Blakely to sit beside me.

In the moments my stalker didn't cloud my mind, I felt free. I felt *naughty*. I knew Blakely hated those moments, but I couldn't help it. He had a natural talent for making me horny.

My skin crawled with excitement at the thought of escaping the city—and its stalker inhabitants—for a week to chat about the publishing industry, and that, paired with my nerves about being alone in my apartment with Blakely, pushed me over the edge.

But let's be honest. Whenever I was alone with Blakely, it didn't take more than a small step to succumb to that edge...

I snuggled closer to him, closing my eyes. I listened to his heartbeat, strong and steady, and the rhythmic motions of each breath. His nose was buried in my hair, and with each exhalation, strands fluttered against my skin, tickling my neck. Quickly, the calming feeling that lingered turned to lust, and my need for him went into overdrive.

I draped a leg over his lap and wrapped my arm around his waist, finding the hem of his shirt. Running my hand against the ridges of his torso, I let my fingers explore, teasing the skin just below the waistline of his jeans. A deep hum escaped his chest. Taking that as a go-ahead, I straddled him, dropping my mouth to his before he could push me away.

With one hand behind my neck and one at the base of my spine, he held me close as he explored my mouth, grazing his tongue against my own with expert strokes. He hardened and lengthened beneath me. I grasped the waistline of his jeans.

My fingers grazed his erection. I brushed them along his hot skin and smiled internally when he groaned in response.

I unbuttoned his pants, but as I worked the zipper, he pushed away, breathless. I was sure the heat in his eyes matched my own. But he stood, lifting me from the seat. He set me down, adjusted, and retreated, slamming his bedroom door shut.

Eventually, he'd cave.

Giving up on getting any action tonight, I attempted to drown my sorrows in alcohol. I poured a glass of lemonade and added a generous splash of vodka. Holding up the glass, I made a silent cheer to Blakely's control before downing the cup and pouring another.

CHAPTER TEN

I stumbled into Blakely's room, tripping over my feet and landing in a thud on the floor. Giggling, I picked myself up and maneuvered through the dark room until I reached his bed. Apparently my stealth-mode wasn't in full gear, because Blakely had sat up in bed, legs dangling over the side as he faced me, by the time I reached him.

He was naked.

"Whoa," I said, swaying as I tried to balance on two feet.

I widened my eyes as I took in the view. When I reached the happy trail of hair that led to the prize, I squinted. In the darkness, the boxer-briefs he wore blended in.

"Oh..."

Damn. He wasn't naked.

I hiccupped and slapped my hand across my mouth to muffle the noise, laughing at my delayed reaction.

"Miss Tate," he said, yawning. "It's late."

I leaned forward, lightly grazing my fingertips across the firm skin of his arm.

"What are you..."

I slipped my arms free of my T-shirt, letting it fall to the floor in a heap.

He inhaled sharply, his eyes trailing down my practically nude frame. I stood in only panties.

"I think you know," I said, running a hand through his tussled hair.

"You're drunk," he said, pushing away my hand.

"I'm tipsy, not drunk. When you're drunk, you can't think clearly, but I can see all the things I want you to do to me with crystal-clear perfection."

I straddled his lap, grabbed his hands, and placed one on each ass cheek. I arched into him, running soft kisses down the curve of his strong jawline. He moaned into my ear.

Oh, yes. He wanted this. He wanted *me*.

"How about we make those dreams a reality?" I whispered.

My nipples hardened as my breasts slid against his soft skin. He dug his fingertips into my flesh and rubbed me against him. He was already hard. I gasped at the contact, my core quivering.

I ran my hands across his chest and linked them behind his neck.

"I want you, Blakely. Here. Now."

In a quick motion, he lifted me, stood, and pushed me up against the wall. My breath caught as I wrapped my legs around him. He closed his eyes and rested his forehead against mine. His breathing was heavy; his heart pounded against me. My nipples ached as they rubbed against the light dusting of hair on his chest. I wanted him badly—just like this. I bit my lower lip at the thought of all the things he could do to me if only he'd let me in.

"We shouldn't do this..."

His eyes were still closed when he spoke, and he shook his head, his skin lightly grazing mine.

"For once in your life, Blakely, don't think about the consequences. Just be here. Now. With me."

His eyes now burned into mine, and I saw the moment he decided to have me. The desire giving way burned brightly within them.

He carried me and laid me down. He climbed onto the bed, planting soft kisses on my skin as he made his way toward me. He slid his hand along my curves, leaving a trail of goose bumps. When he reached my waist, he slid his arm behind my back, and I arched toward him, pushing my skin against his. He kissed the curves of my breasts before pulling away, looking at me.

"Are you sure?" he asked, sincerity in his eyes.

I nodded without hesitation. I needed this. I needed him.

He leaned forward to kiss me. His tongue greedily explored my mouth, and I quivered at the sensations building within me. This man was a god. His kiss, his touch, left me wanting so much more.

I hiked up my legs and pulled down his underwear with my feet, kicking them to the floor. His hand found my panties, and in one swift motion, he ripped them off, tossing the shreds of fabric to the ground. I winced at the sensation. It left my skin raw, vulnerable, and was oddly erotic.

Pulling away, he slid his hand down the length of my stomach. I closed my eyes at the sensation, dragging my teeth against my lower lip.

"Open your eyes, Jezebel."

His voice was calm, controlling. It was an order, and I eagerly obeyed.

Lightly, he brushed his fingertips against the sensitive bundle of nerves that throbbed at my core. I gasped, and his fingers moved lower, reaching my center.

He groaned, his eyes darkening with need.

"You're already ready for me," he said.

He trailed kisses across my collarbone and up the curve of my neck. I gasped.

"I love how responsive you are to me."

"Yes," I whispered, pulling him closer to me and urging his fingers to travel deeper.

His fingers curled within me until they reached a spot so deep, so hidden, I thought no one would ever find it. I dug my fingers into his skin, and he shifted. The palm of his hand rubbed against me while his fingers teased the perfect spot inside me. I closed my eyes, arching my back. His mouth found my nipple and sucked, his tongue playfully stroking the hardened tips. The dual sensation sent me to the edge, and I was begging to fall.

"Come for me, Jezebel."

His breath was hot against my aching breast.

The sound of my name on his lips sent me over the edge.

"Oh, fuck!" I cried out.

My release came in waves, my body stiffening. I dug my fingers against him, holding him tightly until the final wave of release passed. Slowly, I opened my eyes and looked down at him.

"Your turn," I said with a smile, pushing him off me as I straddled him.

He grasped my hips and rubbed his hardened length against me. I rested my hands against his chest, steadying myself against him as another orgasm threatened to consume me. My head rolled back, and my eyes fluttered shut. My wetness coated him as he teased me by gliding my lips up and down his length. The room was dark. I hadn't yet seen him fully nude, but the time it took for him to slide me from one end to the other told me his dick was massive and that this would be the best fuck of my life. It took what little control I had not to arch my hips and let him slip inside.

My core clenched, my legs stiffening. I was close to another release.

"Fuck me. I'm going to come again."

I was breathless, needy, and completely ready to do whatever he asked of me.

"Slowly," he said.

I opened my eyes, confused. Before I could decipher his cryptic message, he angled my hips and rested the tip of himself against my core. I swallowed hard, nodding. Slowly, I lowered myself onto him. Scratching my nails against his skin, I winced at the immediate shock of something so thick entering me.

"Fuck," I whispered.

Sitting up, he stopped me from continuing my descent. He sat there, half in, half out, and brushed away the hair that clung to my forehead. I hadn't realized I'd started to sweat. A single drip trailed down the curve of his cheekbone, and I wondered if the physical exertion was due to the heat, the sex, or our control. We were both breathing heavily as we stared into each other's eyes. I leaned forward and kissed him softly.

"Are you okay?" he asked. His breath was hot on my lips.

I nodded. "I want more. I want all of you." I wiggled my hips, hoping to coax him into me even more.

"Slowly," he repeated.

He released my hips, letting me take back control.

"I don't want it slow. I want it hard, fast. I want to scream."

He smiled as he leaned back until he was flat against the bed.

"Trust me, every inch of me will fuck you tonight, but I'm big, and you're tight," he said, rolling my hips in his hand. "You need to get used to me first."

I bit my lip and continued the slow descent. When he was

finally rooted in me, I shifted my hips and slowly rose from him. Releasing only a few inches, I lowered myself onto him again. I continued to ride him at this ridiculous, agonizing speed until I couldn't take it anymore. I leaned forward, resting both hands against his chest, and quickened my pace. He matched my efforts with quick thrusts of his hips, our chests heaving in unison. I angled my hips, letting him hit that deep spot no one had ever found before.

"Fuck, yes. Right there." I closed my eyes. "Right. There."

He grabbed my hips tighter, pounding into me. His legs tensed beneath me, and I knew he was close to his release.

"Don't stop," I said breathlessly. "Please don't stop."

With one hand leaning against his chest, I grabbed on to my breast with the other, rolling my hardened nipple between two fingers.

"Fuck, Jezebel," he whispered.

I opened my eyes to find him watching me play with myself. I brought my hand to my mouth, slowly sucked on the two fingers, and then grabbed my nipple.

"You like that?" I asked.

He didn't say anything.

"Like it when I touch myself?" I continued.

His muscles flexed as he fucked me harder, seemingly putting everything he had into it. I dropped my breast to steady myself, leaning against him. With his name on my lips, I came long and hard. His release matched mine, and I felt him fill me. I fell forward, resting against him. After I caught my breath, I rolled off him, wincing as he pulled out of me.

I would definitely feel this in the morning.

"That was—" he whispered.

"Incredible," I finished.

He smiled, pulling me closer to him. I snuggled against him, resting my head on his chest. My eyes were heavy, and I was losing my battle to keep them open.

"Sleep with me tonight?" I asked.

He kissed my forehead and covered us with the blankets.

My head throbbed, my core ached, but I had never felt safer or more at peace. I placed a soft kiss on his chest and let darkness consume me.

CHAPTER ELEVEN

I woke to the sound of Manhattan traffic blaring outside the window. Even three stories up, I couldn't escape it.

"Fuck this city," I mumbled.

The throbbing in my head only intensified when I opened my eyes, so I quickly snapped them shut again. A crash in the kitchen had me peeking through my eyelashes. Blakely wasn't in the room, but the smell of breakfast wafted toward me. My stomach grumbled. I craved hangover food even more than I craved last night's dick.

I stumbled into the bathroom, slowly moving through my routine with the lights off. Showering in the dark proved tricky, but I refused to cave. I cursed the invention of the LED lights my eyeballs couldn't handle.

I thought about the millions of people who partied every night. Why would anyone willingly do this *every day*?

Shutting off the water, I plodded into my bedroom, threw on some sweats, and found my way into the kitchen, where Tara was cheerfully making breakfast. Music played from her cell phone, and she shook her hips to the beat. Humming softly, she flipped a pancake into the air and caught it with the pan. I rolled my eyes.

Morning people were really fucking annoying.

I glanced at the clock on the microwave. One thirteen. My jaw nearly hit the floor. I'd slept until one-fucking-thirteen? I scanned the room for Blakely, but he wasn't here. Instead, I found an unlabeled glass bottle filled with a greenish-orange liquid and four brown pills. There were two yellow sticky notes above them. *Drink me. Take me.* I popped the pills into my mouth and took a swig of the juice.

Blech!

The juice was disgusting. I slammed the bottle against the counter, startling Tara out of her dance marathon.

"You're awake!" she yelled.

I winced, throwing up my arms to shield me from her words.

"Quietly," I whispered.

"Yeah, Mr. Blakely said you'd be hung over."

I peeked at her through my lashes. She was shaking her head.

"Save your ridicule, Tara. And what is this shit?" I said, pointing to the bottle of juice.

She shrugged, dropping pancakes onto a plate.

"Some top-secret government hangover cure, I guess."

She scooped some eggs onto the plate, tossed on some bacon, and set the plate in front of me.

"*Bon appétit!*"

I grabbed the fork, took a bite of eggs, and said, "Well, it tastes like ass."

She smiled. "He said you'd say that. He also said to force-feed it to you if you don't drink it willingly."

I rolled my eyes, swallowed my mouthful of food, and took a swig of the disgusting drink.

"He said you should down it quickly, and before you know it, you'll be good as new."

I groaned, plugged my nose, and finished the drink.

"*Yummy,*" I said sarcastically. "So where is Mr. Sunshine?"

She shrugged. "Said he had to run errands."

"Errands?" I questioned.

"He told me to stay here with you and to let you sleep in. Looks like you had a long night, eh?"

I knew that tone. That was her I-have-something-on-Jez tone.

"We fucked."

I figured admitting I had a problem was the first step to her minding her own business.

"I knew it! I found you in his bed, and I knew you slept with him. Honestly, Jezebel, how could you?"

I arched an eyebrow. "Huh. That wasn't nearly as annoying as it should have been. What's in that miracle shit?" I picked up the empty bottle and gave it a once-over. Finding nothing, I set it back down.

"Oh, no, no, no. You're not changing the subject that easily. You slept with him? Have you lost your mind?"

"*Please*, not you too. I don't need another Debby Downer."

"He's your *employee*, Jez. That's sexual harassment!"

Huh. I hadn't thought of it like that. I took a mouthful of pancakes and said, "See, that's why I keep you around. You think of the important stuff." I winked.

"No, I just think with my brain and not my emotions. This was a huge mistake, Jez." She shook her head. "I mean, I'm sure he's not going to sue you—"

"He enjoyed himself. *Trust me*." I brushed away her concern with the wave of my hand.

"That's not the point, Jez, and you know it. I knew hiring him would cause problems. We just need him to keep you alive until we figure out who the stalker is."

"And in the meantime, I'm going to enjoy my guard." I

wiggled my eyebrows as I took the last bite of my breakfast. "Delish as always, Tara. Thanks."

"When this comes back to bite you in the ass, I *will* be there to tell you *I told you so*."

I ignored her as I cleaned up the kitchen, feeling one hundred times better than I had when I woke up. Apparently, Blakely's shit-drink was magic in a bottle.

"Jez?"

I turned after putting the last dish in the dishwasher and wiped my hands on a towel as our eyes met.

"I'm glad you found him," she said.

I dropped the hand towel onto the counter and offered a small smile. "Maybe he found me."

I'd been alone for so long. It was difficult to remember my life before the accident that claimed my parents and my innocence. Now, I was nothing like that girl, and in truth, I hated remembering her. But something about Blakely kept bringing her back to the forefront of my memory.

I wasn't sure why she waited there for me, but I knew, soon, even the comforting safety blanket of time wouldn't stand between us.

CHAPTER TWELVE

Tara had fallen asleep on the couch by the time Blakely finally returned. I smiled at him from the floor, where I sat while we watched yet another *Gilmore Girls* marathon. Tara once told me I was obsessed with this series because of the mother-daughter bond the main characters had. I, too, had had a similar bond with my mom, and this was Tara's way of attempting to get me to talk about her. I'd ignore her pleas to open up while turning up the television's volume.

Noticing Tara snoring softly on the couch, Blakely motioned for me to join him in another room.

"What's up?" I asked when we reached his bedroom.

"How're you feeling?" he asked. He searched my features, as if looking for signs of a lie.

I smiled. "Fine. Your drink tasted like ass, but it worked fairly quickly."

He nodded. "Good."

"No need to check in on me, Blakely. I'm a big girl."

The words escaped me before I thought them through, and truth was, I liked that he cared. The only person who'd cared for me all these years was Tara. I liked knowing I could add another name to that list.

"It's my job to care about your well-being, Miss Tate."

Fuck. He was back to being Mr. Professional.

"I think it's time we were on a single-name basis, Blakely. After all, we did fuck."

His jaw clenched, and I admired the bulge. I'd never been one to notice jaw lines and facial muscles before, but now, every single time Blakely did it, I found it sexy as hell.

"Perhaps we shouldn't broadcast that so loudly."

"Why? Tara knows."

"You told her?" he asked, eyes widening.

"Well, yeah. She's my best friend. Plus, she found me sleeping in your bed. It doesn't take a genius to do that math."

He exhaled sharply, running a hand through his hair.

"Why does it matter?" I asked.

"I prefer it if we kept that aspect of our...*relationship*... between you and me."

"Because?" I crossed my arms over my chest. I couldn't hold back my anger. I kept secrets from the world every day, but suddenly, the thought of keeping Blakely a secret irked me.

"Because until you decide whether you want another bodyguard, I'm all you have. I need to remain focused on your surroundings, not your...assets."

I nodded. "Fine. I'll make sure Tara knows this is 'top-secret' information." I added air quotes for emphasis.

I turned on my heel to walk away, but he caught my arm, pulling me back to him. I stumbled toward him, stopping short of making contact. I glanced up, meeting his gaze.

"Don't read into this, Jezebel," he said.

"How could I? You're not exactly the I-wear-my-emotions-on-my-sleeve type. I never know what you're thinking, so how could I read into this?"

I'd thought after last night, he'd be done playing games.

"Jezebel—"

"I mean, we had sex. What's the big fucking deal?"

"I don't want to argue about this."

"No, you'd rather avoid it. I *know* you want me, Blakely. I can see it when you look at me, when you touch me. Why can't you just admit that?"

"Because if I admit that, this relationship will continue, but it needs to end here."

I stood on my tiptoes. Our lips were only a few inches apart now. "Don't tell me you didn't enjoy it."

Swallowing hard, he said nothing.

"You liked it. You liked fucking me, sliding your dick in nice and slow until you were rooted so fucking deeply I wanted to scream. You liked it when I sucked my fingers and played with my nipples. You liked it when I rode you fast and hard. You liked it when I screamed your name while I came. I fucking rocked your world, and at least one of us can admit it."

I ripped my arm from his grasp, spun on my heel, and began to storm out of his room, but when I reached the door, Blakely wrapped an arm around my waist and pushed me up against the wall. With one hand on my hip, he slid the other under my panties and caressed my core. I gasped, my head rolling back to rest against his chest. He ground his hardening erection against my ass. His breath was hot on my neck.

"Is this what you want?" he asked.

Closing my eyes, I gripped the wall with one hand and the back of his neck with the other. "Yes, please."

He slid a finger between my folds, nearly lifting me off the ground with each deep thrust into my depths. I bit my lip to keep from crying out.

"Don't wake Tara," he said, though it sounded more like an order.

He placed gentle kisses against the curve of my neck before biting down on my shoulder. The stubble on his jaw scratched against my sensitive skin, and I gasped.

"Fuck."

"Tell me what you want, Jezebel."

So many things. I wanted so many fucking things.

I wanted him inside me.

I wanted to taste him.

I wanted him to taste me.

I opened my eyes.

"I want your mouth," I said, leaning forward, resting my forehead against the wall as he continued to fuck me with his fingers.

He kneeled behind me, placing a kiss at the curve of my lower back, and then licked the length of my spine with the tip of his tongue. When he reached my hairline, he bit down softly.

Fuck! This man knew how to arouse a woman.

Much to my dismay, he freed his hand and spun me to face him. With my back pressed against the wall, I watched as he sucked the slickness from his fingers. When he was done, he pulled me into a quick, hard kiss before dropping to his knees. He pulled down my pants, freeing just one leg. I leaned against the wall and balanced on one leg, resting the other against his shoulder. He looked up at me, dragging his teeth against his bottom lip, before turning his attention to my core. I ran my hands through his hair, tugging on the ends and pushing his head against me as his tongue worked me. He licked and sucked and flicked, drawing me closer and closer to the edge.

"Fuck," I whispered, wobbling forward. He grabbed my ass, steadying me. "S-So good."

The stubble of his jaw brushed against my inner thigh. His tongue dipped inside, licking, taunting. He teased me. I needed my release, but I needed it while he was fucking me.

"Blakely," I said, breathless. "I want you...inside."

Leaning against the wall, I grabbed the hem of my shirt and pulled it over my head. I grabbed my breast, squeezing it, tugging on my nipple through the thin lace. I pulled my bra up until it was over my head and then dropped it to the floor.

As much as I wanted him inside me, I couldn't stop my release from consuming me. With each stroke of his tongue, I was one step closer to falling.

"I-I'm... Soon. Fuck! R-Right now. Right now," I said, and my release crashed through me. I couldn't stop myself from free-falling. I came hard, fast, and I couldn't hold myself up anymore. I collapsed in his arms, and he held me there. I was pinned against the wall as he devoured me.

He tossed me over his shoulder and carried me across the room and into his walk-in closet. He set me down and dropped his pants, springing free. I widened my eyes at the sight of him. He was glorious—long, thick, and veiny. I wanted every fucking inch of him inside me again. I trailed my hands along his frame until I met his gaze.

With a cocky grin on his face, he asked, "See something you like?"

I licked my lips, nodding. I got on my knees and wrapped my fingers around him. "I want to taste you."

"As much as I want that, there's no time."

He closed the closet door, locking us inside. I frowned.

"Tara will probably be up soon, but if I'm not inside you in the next thirty seconds, I'm going to lose my fucking mind."

I swallowed hard and relished in his honesty. He wanted me as badly as I wanted him. The only difference was that he had much better control. I stood, wrapped my arms around his neck, and jumped, wrapping my legs around him.

"Are you ready for me?" he asked, resting the tip of his length against my center.

I nodded.

"Don't scream," he said as he sank into me in one quick, long, hard stroke.

A cry escaped my lips, but I quickly muffled it. I scratched at his back as he slid in and out of me in rapid succession. I leaned forward and sank my teeth into his shoulder when the first orgasmic wave hit. After it passed, I released him.

"Yes, fuck. So. Good. Don't. Stop."

He thrust harder and deeper with each word.

"So tight," he whispered. "So good."

I kissed him, tasting myself on his lips, and moaned into his mouth as he rubbed against that perfect spot deep inside me.

"Right there. R-Right there."

"Come with me."

I nodded, resting my head against his forehead. Loose strands of hair clung to our slick skin, but I didn't care. All that mattered was the sensation of him inside me. He felt so perfect, so right. If it was possible to fall in love with a dick, then I was head over heels for Blakely's.

He tensed beneath me, his fingers digging into my thighs, and I knew he was close.

"Ready?" he asked.

I nodded.

He kissed me. It was a long, deep, slow kiss that made my heart ache. When he pulled away, he came. The look on his face, knowing I could give him that much pleasure, sent me over the edge, too. I cried out his name, and we sank to the floor. I rested against him, letting my breath catch, not wanting to return to reality.

When I was with him, the world disappeared. All I could think about was the feeling of his skin on mine. I didn't want to revisit the pain of the world. I didn't want to think about bodyguards and stalkers. I just wanted to stay here with Blakely forever.

But even in the movies, forever never lasted longer than the credit roll.

I sat back and wiped my hair from my eyes.

"So, what does this mean?" I asked.

His smiled faded. "I guess this means you better hire a damn good secondary bodyguard."

I bit my lip. "Why's that?" I leaned closer to whisper in his ear. "Planning to fuck me again, Blakely?" I wiggled my hips.

A deep rumble vibrated in his chest, and he grabbed my hips to steady them.

"Don't tease while I'm still in you, Jezebel. I can go again."

His words were a threat, and I felt that promise to my core.

"You have no fucking idea how sexy you are," I said, standing.

I wobbled, trying to maintain my balance, but my legs felt like jelly. I felt a thick, slow drip slide down the curve of my thigh. Glancing down, I watched its descent.

"That's so fucking sexy," Blakely said.

I bit my lip, silently thanking the inventor of birth control.

★ ★ ★

Taking a seat at a bar stool, I glanced over at Tara, who was still asleep on my couch. I smiled, shaking my head. She was going to be pissed when I told her I had no intention of not fucking Blakely again.

"I have something for you," Blakely said, breaking my concentration. He took the stool beside me as he placed a black jewelry box in front of me.

"Isn't it a little soon to propose?" I joked.

He exhaled dramatically, and I took the hint, opening the box.

The light from the ceiling reflected against the metal of a small, simple, silver cross. I was once a religious person, but after I lost my parents, I cursed the idea of an all-knowing being. How could I believe in a God who'd allow that to happen to his followers? I'd felt abandoned, and I didn't care to relive those feelings.

"It's beautiful," I said, running my thumb against the cool metal.

"There's a GPS tracker in it," he said.

Ah. I should have known.

He slid the box from my hands, pulled the necklace free, and stood behind me, clasping the necklace around my neck. I let it fall. It hung low, resting just above the arch of my breasts.

"The chain's too long," I said.

He shook his head as he sat beside me, and I turned to face him, running a hand over the cross.

"It's meant to hang low. It's not meant for display. I want it hidden."

"Oh..." I said.

The metal was cold against my skin.

"Wear it always, and I'll find you," Blakely promised.

I swallowed the knot that was forming and smiled.

"I trust that you will," I whispered.

He reached forward, brushing a loose hair behind my ear. In that moment, time stood still for us both. But as usual, Blakely pushed me away.

Clearing his throat, he said, "I've been thinking about Maine. We need a cover story."

My interest piqued. "Cover story?"

"We'll attend as partners. That way, no one will suspect anything when I follow you around. They'll think, being new to this relationship, that we're young and in love."

I nodded. A week-long trip away with Blakely as my significant other? Fuck, yeah!

"Sounds good to me. I'll be *all yours*."

His jaw clenched, and I bit my lip at the sight of it. Never had a man made that look so damn sexy.

CHAPTER THIRTEEN

I dropped my suitcase on my bed and filled it with the clothes and supplies I'd set aside for my trip to Maine. We weren't due to leave for another day, but I couldn't stop myself. I was too excited at the idea of a week away with Blakely. I was ready to ride that dick all over the hotel. I wasn't sure what I was more excited about—seeing old friends or fucking Blakely until I couldn't see straight. How the fuck could Blakely have thought pretending to be my boyfriend would be a good idea? That momentary lapse in judgment would work to my benefit, though, so I didn't press the issue.

I zipped up my bag and lugged it into the hallway.

"You're packed already?" Blakely asked, an eyebrow arched.

"Yep," I said, breathless, as I dragged the heavy tote to the front door. I pushed it against the wall, exhaled sharply, and dusted off my hands. "Better to do it now than in the morning. I thought I could make us dinner. I have a chicken casserole ready to put in the oven."

A small smile formed on his face when he nodded. "Sounds good."

A hard knock on my front door startled me. I jumped back, heart pounding, proving, once again, I could never survive writing a horror novel. Blakely, on the other hand, was his usual cool, calm, collected self.

Or not.

He pounced into action, placing himself between the door and me.

"I'm sure it's just a neighbor or Tara," I whispered. Even so, I didn't move.

"Probably," he said, peeking through the small, circular opening in my door. Stepping back, he unlocked and opened the door.

"Mr. Blakely," Tara said as she sidestepped him.

"You need to remember to call or text before you come over, Mrs. Johnson," he said.

I scowled. "No, she doesn't. You're always welcome."

"*Ugh*, I know. I'm sorry. I keep forgetting about these new rules."

I rolled my eyes. "Ignore him. What's up?"

"I just wanted to see you before you go. What time are you leaving?"

"Too fucking early, that's when," I said. It was not a secret that I wasn't a morning person.

"Around seven," Blakely clarified.

"Yeah, like I said. Way too fucking early." I crossed my arms over my chest.

Tara shook her head, laughing. "Some things never change. Well, anyway, I just wanted to make sure you had everything you need. And do you know if you'll have cell service?"

"I'm good, and yeah, I should."

She nodded. "Okay."

She tugged some loose hair behind her ear. Her usually flowing black locks were pulled back into a tight ponytail. Her bright-orange top contrasted against her dark skin. She shifted from foot to foot as she scanned my apartment.

She was nervous, but she'd never admit it. This was the

first time I was leaving the safety of my home for more than a couple of hours, and we were still no closer to discovering the identity of my stalker.

"I'll be fine, Tara. *Trust me.* I'm sure Blakely will never let me leave his side."

She smiled, glancing up at Blakely. "Yeah, I suppose."

I grabbed her arm and pulled her into a hug. "Y'know I love you, right? You're the best friend a girl could ask for, not to mention the best damn lit agent in the game."

She leaned into me, taking deep breaths. "I know, but it's my job to worry."

"Why don't you stay for dinner? I'm making my famous chicken casserole!"

She pulled away, shaking her head. "No, no. I'm fine. Besides, I have dinner plans. I have meetings soon." She glanced at her watch. "Speaking of which, I need to go." She turned to leave, but before closing the door behind her, she shot Blakely a glance over her shoulder. "Take care of her."

And with that, she was gone. The door closed, and Blakely bolted it shut.

I exhaled slowly. I loved Tara for worrying, but I hated how her worries had the ability to make reality come crashing down on me. I decided to ignore those fears while I sauntered into the kitchen.

I slid the casserole into the oven, set the timer, and plopped onto the couch, scrolling the TV for a good time-waste. Finding nothing, I groaned and clicked it off. I scanned the room, letting my gaze settle on my laptop. I hadn't written in a few days. I'd taken a hiatus until the bodyguard search was over, and now that it was, I could get back to my latest novel. I still wasn't sure what I was writing. It happened like that sometimes. I'd sit down to write without truly knowing what I was going to create.

I often found inspiration by walking around the city. I'd camp out somewhere in Central Park and people-watch. The plots of novels played out like movies in my mind. I was lucky, I guess. Not every writer had it so easy.

The couch sank beside me with Blakely's weight, and I smiled, letting myself lean against him.

"I can't decide if I should get back to my book now or wait until we're back from Maine."

"Wait," he said.

I leaned back, and he lifted his arm to let me lean fully against him. "Yeah, I guess. I don't like to take breaks once I've started a new book, but since I'll probably get no writing time at the residency, it would be smart to wait."

"What are you writing about?" he asked.

I shrugged. "It'll come to me. Maybe a sexy bodyguard and his luscious client," I teased.

He ran his thumb along the curve of my cheek, and I closed my eyes, letting myself drift away to the sound of his heartbeat.

★ ★ ★

I woke to the incessant beeping of my stove. I groaned, sulked into the kitchen, and pulled out the casserole. I set out plates, silverware, and glasses and walked through the apartment in search of Blakely.

But he wasn't here.

A knot worked its way from my stomach to my throat.

He was gone.

I was alone.

Had he found me?

I ran back into the kitchen, yanked my phone from my bag, and quickly dialed Blakely's number.

The line went dead.

I swallowed hard and fell to my knees. I leaned against the front door as tears threatened to spill. With shaking hands, I fumbled to dial 9-1-1. In the corner of my eye, I saw a curtain blow as a slight breeze pushed it aside. I dared a peek and found the door to my rooftop deck ajar.

Could he be on the roof?

I crawled over to the door and opened it slowly.

"B-Blakely?" I said. I spoke barely above a whisper. Even if he was up there, he never would have heard me.

I took one step. And then another. When I reached the top, I swallowed hard and opened the door that stood between me and whatever was outside, internally cursing myself for not bringing a weapon of some sort. I chastised the women in horror films, but when it came down to it, I acted just as stupid in stressful situations.

Blakely stood at the far end of the rooftop deck. He faced the skyline, his phone pressed to his ear. I walked toward him, scanning my surroundings with each step.

"I told you to never call me," he said.

The person on the other end must have interjected because Blakely was silent a moment.

"There's nothing left to discuss. Do *not* call me again." He clicked off the phone and dropped it into his pocket. His arms hung at his sides, his hands in white-knuckled fists.

I dried my eyes as I reached him, suddenly embarrassed that I had overreacted. I kicked the debris at my feet, and he turned quickly. Noticing me, he offered a forced smile.

Something was different. *He* was different.

"What're you doing up here?" he asked.

"I couldn't find you," I said, my voice shaky.

"Sorry. I thought you'd be asleep longer."

I nodded slowly. "Everything okay?"

"Of course. Why?"

"You seem...upset. Different."

"I'm fine. Let's get inside. It's not safe for you to be up here."

He still seemed off, but I dropped it. Instead of arguing or demanding answers, I quietly followed him.

My emotions must have gotten the best of me.

I was overanalyzing the situation.

After all, if I couldn't trust Blakely, who could I trust?

CHAPTER FOURTEEN

I didn't understand early risers. I moseyed through my morning ritual, spiting whoever thought it'd be a good idea to have six a.m. wakeup calls. I shuffled down the hallway and kicked my bag. It was still sitting where I'd left it the day before. I glanced up to find Blakely staring at me. He'd stopped mid-drink to witness my internal bickering. His cell phone beeped. Setting down his mug, he read the message and barked out a hard laugh.

"Ugh, can you, like, stop being so fucking happy, Blakely?" I grumbled.

"Tara just texted me. You should read it."

He flipped his phone around. I strained my eyes to focus on the bright white screen.

Give her some coffee.

"Tell her to fuck off," I said. Tara and I had been best friends for years. She didn't need to witness my behavior to know exactly how I'd react to certain situations.

Like Blakely, she was too fucking chipper in the morning.

I picked up Blakely's cup and swallowed down the warm liquid.

"That was mine..." he said.

"Not anymore."

"You can nap in the car."

I rolled my eyes. "Why does *everyone* say that? It's not the same as sleeping in a fucking bed!"

He chuckled. "I'll bring down the bags. You grab another cup of coffee and then meet me downstairs."

I waved him off, grumbling under my breath. I poured coffee into his mug and swallowed it down.

"Don't forget to lock up and set the alarm, sunshine," he said, closing the door behind him.

"I'll show you some fucking sunshine," I mumbled.

It was a vague threat at best, and really, I had no idea what it even meant. But Blakely was ruining my routine. I did my best writing late at night, which meant I usually slept until noon. It never bothered me, but it annoyed Tara, who was an early riser. I had listened to too many lectures about missed meetings. In this line of work, it was typical to have writers with my same routine, yet the business world still wanted—and expected—early morning meetings.

I finished my coffee and rinsed out the mug and pot. And then I grabbed my purse, set the alarm, and left the apartment. Outside, Blakely loaded our bags into the trunk of a black SUV. The windows were tinted black. I could only see my reflection in the glass.

"Where'd you get this?" I asked.

"Rental," he said, closing the trunk.

Before I could reach the passenger door, Blakely was by my side, opening the door for me.

"How chivalrous of you," I said, sliding into the car.

I looked around the vehicle. It had been a long time since I'd been in the passenger's seat of a car. I'd given up that luxury once I'd moved to the city. Blakely climbed into the driver's seat, punched a few buttons on the dash GPS, and merged into traffic.

I loved that this city never slept, which was one of the reasons I'd decided to move here. I wasn't the in-bed-by-ten-and-up-by-six type. I thrived on darkness, on the night. When the evils of the world hid within the shadows, I could pretend they didn't exist. Everything looked so much more beautiful at night. Even skyscrapers danced across the skyline, each window's light twinkling against the blackness.

But it wasn't night anymore. Without the shadows, the dangers of the city were on full display.

"Wake me when we get there," I said, reclining my seat and closing my eyes.

★ ★ ★

I woke to the soft sound of classical music playing. I looked up at Blakely. His eyes were fixed on the road. From this angle, I could see the sharp curvature of his jawline. He swallowed, his Adam's apple bobbing against the taut skin of his neck.

"You're watching me," he said without looking over.

"*How* do you do that?" I asked.

A small smile formed. "You pay me to *do that*."

I shook my head and adjusted the seat to sit forward. Yawning, I asked where we were. As soon as the question escaped my lips, I saw a road sign for Kittery, Maine.

"Kittery? That sounds all sorts of naughty."

Blakely shook his head, grabbed his bottle of water, and attempted to remove the cap with one hand while steering the SUV with the other.

"Gimme that before you kill us both," I said, reaching over. I removed the cap and handed the bottle back to him, watching as he took a swig before returning it to me. "I was out for a while, huh?" I said as I put the bottle back in the cup holder.

He nodded. "How'd you sleep?"

I shrugged. "Fine."

We sat in silence, listening to a classical music station.

"Look in the glove box," Blakely said, eyeing me from his seat.

I wiggled my brows at him when he glanced at me, knowing he'd know I was referring to how sexy he was when he ordered me around. I opened the glove box and squealed as I grabbed the CD case.

"I heard you were a fan."

"*How* did you get this? It's not released yet!"

I clutched the CD, my fingers turning white as I stared at the gorgeous cover. She wore a gray, off-the-shoulder sweater with knitted stitching. Her hair was slicked back, and her lips, stained with gloss, were dark in the black-and-white photo.

"A friend of mine works security for Taylor. When Tara mentioned your obsession with her pop music, I thought I'd give him a call, see what he could do."

I ran my fingers across the black-stained scribble. She'd signed it to me, wishing me well.

"I can't believe you did this for me," I whispered. "You have no idea how much this means to me."

I was never a closeted fan. I'd scream Taylor's lyrics until my throat dried and it hurt to swallow. I loved the way she wrote about love and loss. It was as if she spoke to my soul. When she started her career, she was a country music star, but she dropped that facade as she aged. Like me, she was nothing like the girl she used to be.

"She and I are the same age, y'know. We could totally be

besties. Set that up, will ya?" I joked.

He laughed, and the car fell silent as I inserted the CD into the player. I kept the CD on repeat, learning each lyric. Her words moved me. I felt her anger with her haters, her love for her boyfriend. I could only hope my words evoked similar emotions.

CHAPTER FIFTEEN

I scanned the road. There weren't many people out driving. It wasn't quite one p.m. yet, so it was well outside rush hour. I stared through my tinted window. The front driver's- and passenger's-side windows weren't tinted as deeply as the back ones, but they were still dark enough to make it difficult to see inside. I dragged my teeth across the skin of my lower lip.

I reached over and rubbed my hand against Blakely's lap, making sure to give enough pressure to stroke his dick.

The SUV swerved, and Blakely offered an apologetic wave to the only other car on the road.

"Now who's trying to get us killed?" he asked.

I smiled, unbuckled my seat belt, and shimmied closer to him. I increased my pace, rubbing, squeezing, grabbing his hardening length. With my tongue, I traced the curve of his earlobe.

"I'm hungry," I whispered as I started to unbuckle his belt.

The sexy muscles in his jaw tightened as I unzipped his pants.

"This is a horrible idea. You know that, right?" he asked.

He glanced at me, but his eyes said everything his mouth never would. He wanted this. He wanted me. And he might have wanted it more than I did. I didn't care enough to ask.

I freed him, and his impressive length sprang free. Watching the sunlight hit his glistening tip was almost enough to convince me to give up my night-owl ways. I ran a finger across the pre-come that pooled there and brought it to my mouth. I sucked it off my finger, moaning dramatically in the process.

He exhaled sharply and pushed me away.

"We're not doing this, Jezebel. Not here."

He pushed his dick back in his pants, zipped up, fastened his button, and employed the ten-two hand position on the steering wheel before I could even blink.

What the fuck?

"Seriously. Don't pretend you don't want this. You're hard as fuck. You want your dick in my mouth just as much as I do. Maybe more."

He swallowed hard but said nothing.

I smiled. "So, you're going to ignore me?"

What he didn't know was that I could play this game, too, and I was much better at it.

I shifted back into my seat, pulled the lever, and lay down. At this angle, passersby couldn't see me. I'd opted for shorts and a tank top this morning, which worked to my advantage. I slipped my shorts and panties off and angled my body to watch Blakely's reaction. I knew he liked watching me pleasure myself, so I'd give him the show of his life.

I closed my eyes and imagined Blakely and I were already at the hotel and in my room. I wriggled in the seat at the thought of him taking me there. Running my hand across the soft curves of my neck, I moaned and bit my bottom lip.

"Jezebel," Blakely said in that stern, commanding tone that was so fucking sexy. I could feel his eyes on me, which only incited my desire more.

I arched my back, rubbing my thighs together. My fingers trailed past my collarbone, tickling the curve of my breasts.

My nipples were hard peaks, and I knew the thin cotton fabric of my tank top didn't do much to hide them. So, I pulled the fabric down. My breasts sprang free, much like his dick only minutes earlier. And like his dick, they were needy, silently begging me to tease them.

So I did.

I pushed past the silver cross that lay flat on my chest and grabbed on to my breast. I rubbed the peaks of my nipples between my thumbs and index fingers, groaning as I felt the sensation settle at my core. I was already wet, needy. I ached to have Blakely touch me again, even for a moment. I ran my fingers down the length of my torso and spread my legs as far apart as I could. I wasn't sure if he could see me from his angle, but that didn't stop me from running my fingertip over my core. With one hand still teasing my breast, I rubbed the sensitive bundle of nerves with the other.

I arched off the seat. "Fuck," I whispered. "I need you inside me." I sighed, knowing there wasn't much he could do.

My eyes shot open when he took my nipple in his mouth, his tongue playfully flicking the sensitive nub.

I stared at the ceiling, noticing the trees surrounding us were at a standstill. He must have pulled over or taken an exit just to fuck me.

He pushed a finger inside me.

"Fuck, Jezebel," he whispered, releasing my nipple. "You're so fucking wet."

I nodded, my eyes rolling back as he fucked me with his finger. "So fucking wet for you."

He inserted another finger and curled them up, reaching the special spot deep inside me. He teased me there, rubbing, flicking, and my release was approaching.

His mouth was on my nipple again. While he worked one, I teased the other.

"Keep rubbing your clit," he said, and I obeyed.

I was close, so close. My body tensed as it eagerly awaited the explosion of pure bliss.

"Look at me," he said.

I opened my eyes to find him watching me. His tongue darted out, dancing across my breast.

"Come. Now," he ordered.

That simple command was all it took. I was free-falling, crying out for him. I rode my release until there was nothing left. Breathlessly, I smiled at him, clenching my thighs together in the hope I'd spark another orgasm.

I sat up, glancing around. We were at a truck stop, but there was no one around. The closest semi-truck was across the lot.

"That was the sexiest fucking thing I've ever seen. I just wanted to watch, but I couldn't stop myself from touching you."

"I like it when you touch me," I whispered.

His jaw clenched as he handed me my top. "Get dressed. We need to leave before someone sees you."

"Or we can go in the back." I leaned over, caressing his erection. "I can climb on top, ride you until you can't take it anymore."

He tried to muffle a groan.

I unbuttoned and unzipped his pants, letting him spring free. Before he could object, I leaned down and took him in my mouth.

His breath hitched, and his legs tensed. I knew I had him.

He tasted just as he smelled—minty with a healthy dose

of sex god. I'd never been one for swallowing, but all I could think about was tasting his release. I pumped the base of his cock as I sucked on his tip. His hand scrunched my hair, guiding me to the speed he liked. I tried to take him fully, from tip to root, and felt him arch into me.

"Fuck, Jezebel. You'll make me come," he said.

Uh, that was the plan...

I didn't know how I wanted him—in my mouth or in me. But I knew I wanted him. Badly. And right fucking now. I increased my speed, digging my hand into his pants. I grabbed his balls, alternating between a soft rub and a tight grasp. Again, his breath hitched. He thickened in my mouth, and I knew he was close.

I took him fully once more, and he emptied his release into the back of my throat. Greedily, I swallowed him down, squeezing out the last bits of his essence before pulling away and licking my lips.

He stared back at me, breathing heavily. I ran my hand up his shirt, exploring each ridge of his torso as I went. On my descent, I scratched my nails against him.

"Come in the back with me," I said. Leaning forward, I placed delicate kisses to his neck. "I want to feel you inside me, Mr. James Blakely."

He groaned. He liked it when I used his first name. Honestly, so did I, but that realization was too much to handle. This wasn't supposed to be a relationship. We were just fucking. So I pushed aside those feelings and focused on the burning desire within me. He was my bodyguard and fuck buddy. Nothing more. Nothing less.

As I tried to move back, he pulled me into a kiss. His tongue parted my lips, eagerly searching for my own. I leaned into him, letting him swallow my moans. He reached forward and pulled me onto his lap. Before I could argue that the back seat was more practical, he reached down, pulled a lever, and slid the seat back, giving me more than enough leg space. With the click of one more lever, he leaned back as far as his seat allowed, which wasn't much. I guessed car manufacturers didn't want drivers sleeping on the job.

I angled my hips and slid onto his length in one quick drop.

"Christ, Jezebel," he said, digging his fingers into the soft flesh of my hips.

I rode him fast, hard, the car jerking with every movement. If people didn't know what we were doing before, they sure as fuck did now.

"Oh, fuck," I whispered, already approaching my climax.

But I didn't want it to end just yet. I wanted this moment, this feeling, to last forever.

No one had ever made me feel as good as Blakely did. He knew his way around the female form better than any of my previous lovers. Or maybe I'd just forgotten what it was like. After all, it'd been a while since I'd last fucked someone.

Blakely quickened his pace, yanking me down hard while thrusting upward. Wanting to see his body, I pushed up his shirt, bunching the fabric by his chest. His abdominal muscles flexed each time he sank into me. It was glorious.

This quite possibly could be the best fucking cock ever.

Literally.

I rode him fervently, like an explorer lost at sea who suddenly found land. I leaned forward, closing my eyes while resting my forehead against his. I felt his hot breath against my lips, and I craved to kiss him.

"Fuck! I'm gonna come," I said.

I couldn't hear anything except the rapid beat of my heart and the quick bursts of each breath.

Maintaining his speed, Blakely shifted slightly and pressed his thumb against my clit. His touch was firm—rough, even.

"Come, Jezebel," he said, his voice strained, weak.

We came in unison, riding out the ecstatic wave together. When we'd finished, I rested against him, letting my heartbeat slow. Once I'd caught my breath, I sat back.

How did we get here? How did we get to this? Blakely wanted no part in an illicit affair, but I'd pushed him into it. Was it simply my power of persuasion? Was I a better fuck than I gave myself credit for? Or was he developing feelings for me, too?

I lifted my hips, and he slid out of me, his length quickly deflating. I tumbled into my seat, laughing at how ladylike it must've looked.

Ladylike? Who was I kidding? I had just fucked my bodyguard in a rest-stop parking lot. I wasn't exactly going for the crown.

CHAPTER SIXTEEN

We cleaned up and dressed quickly, saying nothing. Blakely pulled onto the road, avoiding my glances.

What was up his ass? This wasn't exactly the first time we'd fucked.

The rest of the ride was awkward. Blakely ignored my attempts at small talk, so I eventually gave up altogether. Lost in my thoughts, I said nothing until after we'd reached the hotel in Portland. Blakely brought in our bags as I checked in. The front desk manager welcomed me and assured me he'd given us his best room. I eyed Blakely curiously. I didn't care about having the best room, but still, I thanked the manager. We took the elevator to our fifth-floor room.

"Did you request the best room?" I asked.

He shook his head.

"Well, then, that was weird."

Blakely looked lost in his thoughts as we exited the elevator and walked down the hall until we found room 503.

I inserted the card key, and we filed in. Blakely dropped our bags on the bed as I looked around. The room was nice, spacious. A small entryway opened to the rest of the room, which housed a seating area, desk, and bed. Speaking of which, there was only one bed. That made sense, of course, since we were supposed to be a couple.

I could already tell this was going to be one fucking awkward weekend trip.

"I can sleep on the chair," Blakely said.

I rolled my eyes. "Really? I think we can share a bed."

He didn't argue.

I found the agenda on the bedside table, and I browsed it.

"There isn't much planned for me, really. There's a formal dinner tomorrow night, and my lecture is the following afternoon." I scanned the other events. "There are some great lectures planned that I might attend."

He nodded, walked into the bathroom, and closed the door.

I exhaled sharply, annoyance building. If this was a good representation of this weekend, then no one would ever believe we were a couple. I stormed toward the bathroom and yanked open the door. I found him leaning against the counter, arms crossed, a dark look in his eyes. He didn't look up as I barged in.

"No one is going to believe we're madly in love if you can't even look at me."

He glanced up, locking eyes with me to prove a point, I was sure.

I took several steps toward him, and he tensed as if I'd struck him. I ignored that and pressed on. "Will it be that difficult to at least *pretend* you like me?"

He let out a sharp laugh. "Pretend? We aren't pretending anymore."

I wasn't ready to talk about my increasingly growing attraction to him. I still wasn't sure what those feelings meant. Every chance they'd had to surface, I'd pushed them down and jumped on his cock.

"I don't... I don't know what you mean."

He closed the space between us and looked down at me.

"We're not just fucking anymore, and you know it."

I swallowed hard and said, "That's all it is to me. You're just a good fuck."

Pain flashed behind his sapphire eyes before they grew dark, cold.

"You can lie to yourself all you want, but I'm not an idiot. This is exactly what I was trying to avoid. Friends who fuck don't work out. This needs to end before someone gets hurt... or worse."

"Or worse? What the fuck is that supposed to mean?"

"Jezebel," he said, his voice softening, "I can't do my job. I can't protect you like this. I can barely focus. I just fucked you in a car, at some dirty rest stop, while an unknown assailant stalks you, for Christ's sake!"

"So, you're leaving me?" I asked softly.

"We're not together, Jezebel. This was strictly a professional relationship."

"I know. I just, I mean, you're quitting? Things get...fuzzy, so you just quit? What happened to Mr. Loyalty?"

"Loyalty left the minute my dick entered you. You and I both know it. I'll stay until you find another bodyguard, but after that, I should leave. It's what's best for your situation."

Tears burned behind my eyes. Why did this hurt so badly? Why did I have to care this much?

"This is exactly why I avoid relationships and stick with Mr. Dependable."

I stormed out of the bathroom, grabbed my bag, and stomped toward the door.

"Mr. Dependable?" Blakely asked as he walked out of the bathroom.

"Yeah. My fucking vibrator that hasn't been used since

you arrived. Looks like he's back to work."

I opened the door, only to have it slammed shut. Blakely was behind me, pinning me to it.

"You can't just storm off. I have to be with you at all times when you leave the room."

"I'm not leaving. I'm getting another room."

I spun around to face him. I was still encaged by his arms, pushed up against the door.

"So, if you'd kindly get the fuck out of my way, I can get another room before they're all taken."

He exhaled slowly. "You agreed, Jezebel. You agreed that you'd listen to me, do what I ask."

"I'm doing just that, *Mr. Blakely*. I'm keeping this a professional fucking relationship."

"I'm not letting you go, Jezebel. Not until you remember the terms agreed upon."

I leaned forward, angling my head back so I was just a few inches from his face. "Fuck your rules, and fuck you!"

He reached back and grabbed a fistful of hair at the base of my neck, tugging it slightly. I gasped at the display of dominance. His jaw was clenched shut, and his eyes were dark.

"What's the matter, Mr. Blakely? Can't handle a woman who stands up to you?"

His breath was hot on my skin, and I could feel his growing erection against my stomach. My defiance was turning him on, but I didn't know if he'd act on it.

I reached down and rubbed his length. "I thought you didn't want me anymore," I whispered.

He leaned down, grazing his lips against mine, and I shut my eyes instinctively. I waited for it, for the kiss that would take my breath away.

But it never came.

When I opened my eyes again, the darkness in his had disappeared. In its place was that broken man I'd seen the day I'd hired him. I had almost forgotten that flash of vulnerability he displayed when I asked him about his family.

He blinked, and the broken man before me was gone. In his place was the alpha—the sexy-as-fuck alpha.

He still held my hair in his palm. I gasped when he tugged it ever so softly. "You will listen to me, Jezebel."

"Or what?" I whispered.

He swallowed hard, jaw clenching. But he said nothing.

"What if I like to be naughty?" I teased.

Instead of responding, he released me, backing away. He grabbed my bag and tossed it onto the bed.

"Here's what's going to happen," he began. "We are going to pretend we're together *in public only*. We are going to sleep *separately* in this room. We're going to stop fucking. And you are going to do whatever I say whenever I say it. Do you understand?"

His tone was forceful, commanding, and it sent a spark of desire straight to my core.

I bit my bottom lip. "I love it when you take charge."

"And you're going to stop making this so damn difficult for me."

I smiled. "I can't make any promises."

He exhaled deeply. "I need you to follow these rules, Jezebel."

"Don't worry, lover. I'll follow your rules. But be honest. Do you *really* think you can stay away? Just admit that you want me as much as I want you."

"I'll unpack," he said, turning toward our bags.

His silence said everything I needed to know. He had no idea that he'd just made the first move of a game I was much better at. After all, I was a romance writer. Seduction was a game I knew all too well.

CHAPTER SEVENTEEN

We entered the elevator to descend to the lobby. I was going to be on the lookout for familiar faces, even though I knew not everyone had arrived. Today was considered a lazy day, one where people slowly trickled in as their flights landed. My alma mater offered a renowned program. People from all over the world applied to learn from some of the best writers in the industry.

I still remembered getting my acceptance call. It had been my final semester of undergrad, and I had been studying for finals in the library when my phone started buzzing. I never answered calls from numbers I didn't know, so I'd let it go to voice mail. But deep inside, something had sparked.

What if that had been *the call*? The one that said, "Hey! I know you have no idea what you plan to do with your life and that English degree, but since you have no desire to teach, why don't you mosey over here and check out this pretty piece of paper? That's a Master of Fine Arts degree, and it would look fan-fucking-tastic on your wall, am I right?"

When I'd listened to the message and heard the voice of Margaret Cooper, the MFA program director, I was floored. I'd been accepted.

"Are you sure?" I'd asked when I called her back. "I'm Jezebel Tate. Maybe there's another Jezebel you meant to call."

She'd laughed and assured me there was no mistake. And

that I had been the only candidate who had received a call directly from her.

I ended up graduating at the top of my class.

The elevator reached the lobby, and Blakely and I exited hand in hand into a crowd. I was introduced to more people than I could ever remember.

I often forgot that being a writer was a form of celebrity. I never cared to partake in that life, and when I did attend a signing, I always felt overwhelmed. Random strangers would hug me, ask for my autograph, and take pictures with me.

Since my parents' accident, I'd built a permanent bubble around myself. I kept out everyone but Tara, and I cringed when someone invaded my personal space.

For the quickest of seconds, my mind flashed to the stalker. Had my bubble protected me from him? If I had been as open as some authors, maybe he would have found me sooner.

I continued introducing myself to new faces, and then I heard a familiar voice.

"Jezebel, I'm so happy you accepted our invitation!"

I shrieked, spinning on my heel. "Of course, Margaret! I'm so happy to be back."

I pulled her into a long, tight hug. I rested my head in the nook of her neck and inhaled deeply. She smelled like home. We had grown close after her acceptance call. She'd learned of my history, and never having children of her own, she'd checked in on me regularly. I'd worried her. Hell, I'd worried everyone. I had been high on caffeine and alcohol and detached from my emotions for years after my parents' death. I released her and stepped by Blakely's side.

Showtime.

He wrapped an arm around my waist, holding me close. I

looked up at him, smiling widely.

"Blakely, I'd like you to meet Margaret Cooper, the program director. Margaret, this is Blakely, my boyfriend."

She shook his hand. "It's so nice to meet you, Blakely."

Her tight, curly black hair bounced as she spoke. Her skin was paler than usual, her frame gaunt.

He nodded. "Please, call me James."

Blakely eyed me cautiously.

Shit. I guess it wasn't normal to refer to your partner by his last name.

"I'm so happy you came with Jezebel," Margaret said.

"I don't think she'd let me stay away. She's quite proud of her time here, and she wanted to share that part of her life with me," he said.

Margaret laughed. "Well, fabulous! Are you staying for the entire residency?"

"I'm not sure. I have a hefty publishing schedule this year," I said. "But I will try."

She smiled. "You know, we're so proud of you. I can't open a magazine without seeing your face!"

I frowned. "Really?" I had no idea I was followed so closely by the media. How was that even possible? I rarely left my apartment.

She brushed away my concern. "Oh, it's all rubbish. They spread rumors about stalkers and affairs and things like that. You don't need to worry yourself with it."

My heart sank. So, everyone *did* know. Since losing my parents, I had been able to perfect a particular survival skill set, and removing myself from the world was part of that skill. I never watched the news. I only used the internet for research purposes. And I avoided the tabloids like eight a.m. meetings.

Blakely, who still held me with an arm at my waist, gave me a reassuring squeeze.

"Yeah, well, don't believe everything you read," I said unconvincingly. My tone was breathy, unsure. I waited for her to question it.

But she didn't.

"Did you get a schedule?" she asked.

I nodded.

"The press conference was conveniently missing from the original schedule."

"Convenient?" Blakely questioned.

She laughed. "Writers hate the press."

I nodded. I had forgotten the press would be here. Since this program kept major players on staff, the press often attended the residency with the hopes of getting interviews.

"Anyway, it's tomorrow. A revised copy of the schedule should be at the concierge desk."

"I can't wait," I said sarcastically.

"Margaret!" someone yelled.

Margaret explained she'd chat with us later before disappearing in the crowd.

"Well, wasn't that fun," I said, pulling away from Blakely.

Suddenly, I needed to get away. The room was too small, the people were too many, and the drinks weren't going to be strong enough.

"Just breathe, Jezebel," he said. "You'll be fine. You handled that well."

I nodded, eyeing the bathroom door. "I need to pee."

I practically ran toward the door, pushing it open with such force it slammed against the wall. In here, I was alone. I rested my palms against the cold stone countertops and stared at myself in the mirror. My skin was flushed. I turned on the water, wet my hand, and rubbed the cool liquid against the back of my neck.

Before we'd left the room, Blakely and I had both changed. He'd opted for dark jeans and a black Henley shirt. I thought it would be funny to match him, so I wore a dark top and black skinny jeans. But now, I regretted it. My flushed skin was blaring back at me, mocking my attire decisions.

I took several deep breaths and made my way toward the door.

Leaving the safety of the bathroom, I scanned the room. More and more students, staff, and press were arriving. I smiled and offered courtesy nods as I made my way toward Blakely, who had been cornered by half a dozen people.

"Can you talk about your relationship with Ms. Cox?" a woman asked him. She held her cell phone in hand, eagerly waiting for Blakely to make every newbie's mistake.

Blakely ignored her and instead kept his eyes on me as I approached. He offered an apologetic smile as I stepped beside him.

"Ms. Cox! I'm a huge fan," she gushed. "I absolutely love your western novels. I was never a fan of cowboys until I read your books." She winked.

"Me neither."

She barked out a hard laugh and snorted. Her eyes grew wide, her cheeks reddened, and she excused herself.

"Ms. Cox, I'm with the university's paper. We'd love to interview you, talk about your success since graduating."

He was young, clearly still a student. His eyes were hopeful, full of promise.

I smiled. "Absolutely."

Biting the bullet was the best approach. After all, interviews were part of the job, and I couldn't think of a better interviewer than my alma mater's paper.

"Oh, fantastic. When would be best for you?"

"How about now." I forced a smile.

"Yes, perfect! Let me just stop by my room and get some things, put my bags down, and I'll be back." He glanced at his watch. "Just give me five minutes."

I nodded. "Sounds good." He nearly skipped away in retreat.

"I'm surprised," Blakely said.

I glanced up at him. "About?"

"You agreed to an interview."

"It's for the university paper. That's different."

He nodded but didn't speak.

"They're...not as bad as major press reporters. Plus, this will fulfill Tara's interview quota for the month. She sends me interview requests almost daily. I get so many I've considered adding any email with 'interview request' in the subject line to my block list."

Blakely laughed, and I nudged him.

"You think I'm kidding..."

"Oh, no. I know you're serious."

"Hi there," someone said.

I watched a hand reach forward and take Blakely's into a firm grasp. I locked eyes with the man. He was tall, only a few inches shorter than Blakely, and muscular. His frame was a stocky build, whereas Blakely's was lean. His dirty-blond hair washed out his light-gray eyes.

"I'm James. This is my girlfriend, Jezebel Cox," Blakely said, turning toward me.

"Your girlfriend," he said curiously. "Well, then, nice to meet you. Brent Miller."

I smiled and grasped his hand.

A bag was slung over his shoulder.

"Are you a student?" I asked, crossing my fingers. I couldn't handle another press interaction.

He barked out a hard laugh. "No, not at all. I'm with the press. I'd be lying if I said I wasn't delighted to see your name on the lecture list," Brent said. "I was hoping I could sit down with you at some point. Perhaps a drink? My treat."

He offered me a dazzling white smile that I was sure made all the ladies swoon. He was an attractive man, after all.

"I'm sorry, Mr. Miller, but—"

"Please, call me Brent," he interjected.

I cleared my throat. "Brent, I'm sorry, but I won't be giving any interviews. I'm here as a courtesy to the director. I'm not here to make career advances."

I could only hope Brent Miller wasn't eavesdropping when I agreed to an interview mere minutes ago.

"How about an off-the-record talk, then?"

I hesitated, thinking about the likelihood that he'd back down. I hated reporters.

I smiled. "Maybe."

"Great! How about tonight? People will still be coming in, so there will be fewer distractions. We could meet in the restaurant bar." He glanced at his watch. "Seven o'clock?"

I exhaled slowly. "Sounds good."

He smiled brightly, nodding to me as he walked away and disappeared up the stairs.

"Thanks for joining in," I said, elbowing Blakely's ribs.

"It seemed like you wanted to handle that on your own."

"I fucking hate the press."

CHAPTER EIGHTEEN

I didn't change for the meeting with Brent. I didn't see the point. I was going to kindly tell him to fuck off—in a most ladylike way, of course.

I walked into the restaurant, briefly closing my eyes to take in the familiar scent. It didn't matter how many years went by... This place never changed. The restaurant had a wilderness theme. It was, after all, located in Maine. Its walls looked like the inside of a log cabin and were spotted with the occasional stuffed animal carcass. If I were anywhere else—anywhere but Maine, the king of the outdoors, that is—I'd be grossed out. The owner did manage to give it a classy look, though, and that helped.

The room was filled with empty tables as I strode in, my heels clunking against the hardwood floors. I took a seat at the bar beside Brent.

"What'll you have, miss?" the bartender asked as he placed a small, square napkin in front of me.

"A Manhattan, please. And a beer. Whatever's on tap."

He nodded, poured the drinks, and placed them before me, sliding another napkin square under the second drink.

Brent arched a brow, eyeing my two drinks.

"I'm not alone," I said as Blakely walked into the room.

He strode over confidently, taking the stool beside me. He placed a hand on my thigh, giving it a gentle squeeze. Brent watched the movement, an intense glare in his eyes. In a second, it was gone. He lifted his drink.

"To free press, without which, I would not be sitting here with you fine people."

I resisted the urge to roll my eyes at the mention of the press.

"Hear, hear."

I took a sip of my cocktail, relishing the familiar tingle as the cool liquid emptied into my stomach. I felt the burn of alcohol the entire way.

"So, Mr. Miller, where do you do business?" Blakely asked.

"Oh, you know, here and there. Wherever I can find a story, really." He smiled and took a swig of his whiskey. "How about you?"

"New York," Blakely responded.

He nodded. "Yes, of course. Many writers end up there."

"I'm not a writer," he clarified.

"But your girlfriend is."

I couldn't help but notice the way Brent emphasized "girlfriend."

Jealous much?

"What line of work are you in, Mr. Blakely?" Brent asked.

"Military," he answered simply.

"Oh, interesting. How'd you two meet?" Brent pried.

"Enough," I said. "You're not making me into your next story, Mr. Miller. I agreed to have a drink." I threw back the rest of my cocktail, cringing internally as my eyes watered from the rush of alcohol entering my system. "And now I've done just that. Have a good night." I stood and faced Blakely.

Blakely grabbed his beer in one hand and my hand in the other, and we left.

It didn't take us long to reach our room. I kicked off my heels, giving myself a good shudder as I thought about the reporter sitting downstairs.

"He's probably pissed," I said. "No doubt, he'll write some slamming article on me now."

I was horrible at PR. I guess that was why Tara was semi-accepting of my reclusive lifestyle. The more I stayed inside, the less likely I was going to fuck up outside.

"Ignore him."

I heard the door lock latch, and I turned on my heel.

"Let's get drunk," I said, a sly grin forming.

"Jezebel..."

I opened the minibar and found dozens and dozens of mini bottles of alcohol. "Score!"

Blakely shook his head in disapproval. "I'm going to change."

I heard the bathroom door shut, and I dove in. I had to work quickly. He'd only be gone for a few minutes. And I preferred to get drunk without disapproving stares and annoying lectures.

One by one, I opened a bottle, drank down the cool liquid, and let the alcohol do what it was supposed to—erase a shitty memory. After half a dozen drinks, I was beginning to feel *good*. I giggled as I glanced up at Blakely, who scowled down at me. I'd camped out in front of the minibar, and there were empty bottles piled in front of me.

"Want one?" I asked, hiccupping.

"No, and neither do you."

He helped me up.

"I'm not drunk," I said. "Just a little tipsy. Calm down."

I pushed away from him, suddenly feeling the weight of

the last few days on my shoulders. With closed eyes, I rubbed my neck, noticing the muscle tension. I frowned and pushed harder. A moan escaped my lips. I felt him move closer to me and place a hand to the back of my neck. He worked out the knots, and I arched back, pressing my greatest asset against him.

"Jezebel... Remember what I said. This needs to stop."

I reached back, running a hand through his hair. The strands were silky, tickling the soft skin between my fingers. I pulled him closer to me, and he placed a few gentle kisses to the arch of my neck. I moaned in approval.

He stepped back, and I nearly fell on my ass.

"I don't get you. You're hot then cold, hot then cold. And why's it matter? You're going to leave me anyway. Why not get in a few more good fucks?"

I stormed into the bathroom, stripped, and turned on the tub. I emptied the three containers of travel-size shampoo bottles the hotel provided into the water and got in. Leaning back, I was lost in my thoughts.

"Shit," I said, leaning forward and turning off the water as the bathroom door opened.

Blakely entered, his eyes hooded, dark. He undressed slowly. I watched each muscle flex as he pulled his shirt over his head, kicked off his shoes, slid off his jeans and boxer-briefs, and yanked off his socks. He stood before me, gloriously nude. I sucked in a sharp breath. Biting my lip, I drank him in, letting my eyes scour every delicious inch of him. I'd never been one to form fetishes, but if it were possible to form a fetish of a person, then I had a bad fetish for Blakely. I wanted him any way I could take him.

He stepped into the soaker tub. I shimmied forward, and

he sat directly behind me. I leaned against him, loving how my frame nestled perfectly against his. He rubbed every inch of my body his long arms could reach, starting with my neck and back before moving to my chest and stomach. When he reached my arms, my head rolled back, and I peered up at him.

Without drinking more, I was losing my buzz. Thankfully, I could get drunk on just the sight of him.

"Why is it so hard to stay away from you?" he whispered against my forehead before placing a soft kiss against my skin.

"Tell me about it," I replied.

We sat in silence, massaging the parts of each other's bodies that our palms could reach, until our skin wrinkled and the water turned cold.

CHAPTER NINETEEN

The heat of the morning sun against my skin woke me. I opened my eyes to find Blakely sitting beside me, his back resting against the headboard and a laptop sitting on his thighs. He was frowning at the screen. His eyes were cold, dark, distant.

"Morning," I said quietly.

He blinked several times and looked down at me. "Sleep well?" he asked, reaching over to brush hair from my eyes.

I nodded, shivering at his touch.

I glanced at the computer screen. I couldn't see more than the website's header image before Blakely slammed the laptop closed. He tossed the blankets aside and strode to his bag, dropping the computer into its case before zipping it up.

"Everything okay?" I asked.

He nodded.

I grabbed my phone and went into the bathroom, locking the door behind me. Leaning against the counter, I searched for the website. It only took a couple of Google searches until I landed on the personal blog *Living Light: The Untold Story*.

The home page was full of blog entries that dated back several years. I clicked on the website's About page. The blogger was young—around my age. She might have been a few years older. Her name was Abigail. She stared back at me in a staged photo. Everything about her was pale—her skin, her ginger hair, her blue eyes. According to her bio, the Living

Light tragedy led her to start the blog. She wanted to tell the true story behind her parents' involvement in the Living Light Massacre.

My heart sank.

Why was Blakely on this site? Was he somehow connected to this event?

I scrolled through the blog's feed, hoping to find a summary, but there was nothing, and I didn't have time to spend hours reading through her posts. At least, not right now.

I needed to find out what happened straight from Blakely, but I guessed he wouldn't easily give up his history. When I mentioned his family, he became distant. The pain he felt over the loss of his parents was something we shared. I could make him understand that. Maybe then he would tell me what happened.

Eager to find out, I rushed through my morning routine, and when I was done, Blakely was waiting for me.

I smiled at him. "Ready for breakfast?"

★ ★ ★

The hotel's dining room was large, considering they had an on-site restaurant. We entered through the French doors, and all eyes fell on me. I felt my cheeks heat, my heartbeat rise. I was used to being unknown. When I walked the streets of Manhattan, I was invisible to those around me. No one stared. No one knew I was a famous writer. But here, everyone knew me. I swallowed down the lump that was forming.

As if feeling my anxiety level rise, Blakely placed a hand on my lower back, guiding me to an empty table. We sat, and a waitress strolled over.

"Hi there! Would you like the breakfast buffet?" she asked, her curly blond hair bobbing as she greeted us.

"Yes, please, and some coffee," I said.

Blakely asked for some juice while I scanned the room.

My graduate program was a low-residency program, which meant I could enjoy living in Manhattan and only travel to Maine twice a year. During those twice-yearly residencies, the hotel was booked solid. Students cluttered every corner of every room—from the bedrooms to the restaurant to the conference rooms, where lectures were held. Everyone here was either a student, attending lecturer, or with the press.

I cringed at the thought. I knew I'd run into Brent again, and I was dreading it. Columnists were relentless.

"Ready to go up?" Blakely asked.

I nodded quickly.

By the time we'd returned to our table, the waitress had brought our drinks.

With each bite, I scanned the room. Chew. Scan. Swallow. Repeat. It took mere seconds to perfect the routine. I took a sip of my coffee and glanced at Blakely. He too scanned the room with each bite. I wondered if I looked as paranoid as he did when I did it.

"So," I said, and he looked at me. "What do you want to do today?"

He shrugged.

"There's a formal dinner tonight, but after breakfast, I thought I could show you the town."

He nodded, swallowing down a forkful of eggs.

I glanced around, trying to see the world as he saw it. There were many open tables. I guessed that was what happened when you waited until ten to have breakfast. No one sat at the tables beside us. In fact, the only other people in the room were in our direct line of sight, because Blakely had chosen a corner table that had been positioned beside two adjoining walls. I hadn't noticed his choice when we entered the room, but I understood now. It was the safest table in the room. There were no windows in this corner, so no one could greet us from behind. I glanced back at Blakely, noticing his posture. One hand held his fork, and the other rested on his thigh. Looking closer, I could see a slight bulge in his shirt. Was he carrying a weapon?

I shook away the thought. Of course he was armed. He probably had an entire artillery under his clothes. After all, he was being paid to protect me.

Someone barked out a hard laugh. The woman caught my attention. She was with an older man and a young girl. The child was decorating the top of a black graduation cap. Proudly, she dropped the glittery pen and held up the cap. The woman told her it was beautiful and that she would cherish it forever.

I cleared my throat and stared at my food. I had forgotten that a graduation ceremony was held during each residency and that it was a time to celebrate with family. That was an experience I'd never had. My heart ached at the thought, and I clenched shut my jaw in response. I'd buried those feelings long ago and didn't want them to rise again.

I glanced at Blakely and found him watching me. The pain I'd once seen there lingered behind his eyes.

In that moment, I decided to be brave. "Tell me about your family," I said.

The muscles in his jaw ticked. He looked away. I reached forward and placed my hand atop his, giving him a reassuring squeeze.

I'd never wished to discuss the accident that killed my parents, but something about this place, about being here with Blakely, made me want to tell him my story.

It was now or never, because I knew this sudden courage would soon fade into the nothingness I'd felt for so many years.

"Mine were killed when I was in college," I said softly.

His breath hitched.

I exhaled slowly. "It happened only about a month before I was accepted into this program. The only thing that got me through it was knowing my mom would have been so proud of me. We had a small family. After my grandparents died, it was just my mom and dad. They didn't have siblings. They never went to college."

Tears threatened to spill, but I held them back. My eyes were burning at the sensation.

It'd been so long since I spoke of them aloud, since I shared that part of my soul with someone. Once I finally reopened the wounds, everything spilled out.

"It's my fault," I whispered. "I killed them."

The words slipped from me without permission, and the world around me grew dark. What had I just said? I'd never admitted my involvement in my parents' death to anyone. Ever. A wave of nausea rushed over me. I yanked my hand from Blakely's, dropped my fork, and ran from the room. I vaguely heard Blakely calling after me.

I took the stairs two at a time until I reached the fifth floor. It was coming, and I couldn't stop it. I fumbled with the key to the door and had barely pushed it open before running into the bathroom, expelling the contents of my stomach. When I was done, I sat back, wiping the residue from my mouth with the back of my hand. The room was silent save for my heartbeat, and each *thump* was a suffocating reminder of my survival.

After having a better grasp on reality, I stood on shaky legs and made my way to the sink to splash water on my face and brush my teeth. When I exited the bathroom, I found Blakely sitting on the edge of the bed.

"Jezebel," he said. He looked...defeated. "Tell me what happened."

I shook my head, another wave of anger, sadness, and disgust threatening to overtake me.

"What did you mean when you said you killed them?"

His voice was calm, collected. He spoke to me like he was a homicide detective in an interrogation room. I felt judged, and that made me angry.

"They died because of me!" The words burst from my chest. "Finals were coming up, and I couldn't deal. So I went to a party on campus, and I got drunk. I called my parents for a ride. On the ride home, while we fought about responsibility and the danger of getting wasted at a party with guys I didn't know, we got into a car accident. A drunk driver crossed the median and hit our car head-on."

The tears no longer threatened me. Instead, they were staining my white shirt with light-gray blotches as I sank to my knees before Blakely. I stared up at him, focusing on his figure through my blurred vision.

"I can still see it all so vividly. I can hear the screech of the tires as the driver tried to stop, and my mom...she's screaming. I looked up, and I was blinded. The headlights burned. They were so bright...too bright. I can smell the stench of vomit in my mouth as my dad tried to swerve away from the truck. I'm not— I'm not supposed to remember! You don't remember this well"—I dug my hands through my hair, scratching at my scalp—"when you're sloppy drunk. This...this is my p-punishment. Don't you see?

"And then, it hit us. My head slammed against the window, and suddenly, the world fell silent. My mom wasn't screaming anymore. The car wasn't swerving away. I was free-falling until the car skidded to a stop. I opened my eyes, and...

"I can feel... I can feel the glass in my hair, digging against my skin. Everything hurts, and I can smell th-the burnt rubber, but that's n-nothing compared to the blood. Oh, God. It's everywhere. It's all around me. It's on my skin. It's on the windows. It's in the air. I can't— I can't smell anything else. I just... I just want to smell the rubber again." I'm feeling nauseated, and I know I'm going to throw up again, but I swallow it down.

"I try to call out, but I can't. I can't call out to her, to my mom, to my dad. I can't tell them I'm okay. I can't tell them to hold on. Before the accident...sh-she kept nagging, and I was starting to feel sick. I told her— I told her I hated her. I hated that she was ruining my buzz. That's the last thing I ever said to her. That I hated her."

I released a terrifying bellow—a noise even I hadn't known I could create. In it, I expressed the emotions I'd held on to for so many years—pain, longing, regret, despair.

"It was my fault. They w-wouldn't be dead if I hadn't drunk that night. I k-killed them. I killed my parents."

I dropped my head against my palms and let it out. I hadn't heard Blakely join me on the ground, but when he pulled me onto his lap and held me tightly, I didn't fight him.

"It wasn't your fault, Jezebel."

"Stop it!" I said, trying to push away.

He shushed me and, again, told me it wasn't my fault.

That it would be okay.

"No! Stop!" I yelled between hiccups. "Please, tell me I was wrong, tell me it was my fault. P-Please don't forgive me."

I buried my head in the crook of his neck, releasing the pent-up anger and guilt that had been buried for years. Eventually, the tears stopped, and all I could do was listen to Blakely tell me it wasn't my fault.

He repeated that sentiment over and over until I wondered if he might be right. After all, he wasn't the first to tell me that.

I'd known Blakely for mere days, yet he was able to completely break down the wall I'd spent a great deal of time building.

But the wall surrounding me was only the beginning. Behind it, I was left in pieces, waiting for the day I'd become whole again.

CHAPTER TWENTY

After I calmed down, I glanced up at him. He rubbed a thumb along the curve of my jawline and placed a kiss to my forehead. The darkness that occasionally haunted him stared back at me in his eyes. His secrets were there, and it was as if they were begging me to make the first move, to help release them from their captor.

"Tell me about your family," I whispered.

His eyes were empty pits of despair. I fought the urge to pull him close, because shutting down, ignoring the past, wasn't helping either of us. He swallowed hard and exhaled slowly. His arms fell to his sides, releasing me from his embrace.

"I grew up in a self-sufficient religious community called Living Light. I was born there. Have you heard of it?"

Again, his eyes remained on the empty space before him.

I wondered if I should tell him that I caught a glimpse of his website searches. I decided to lie. If he knew, he'd stop to think about what this moment meant. I needed to tell him about my past mistakes—just like I was sure he needed to release his, too.

"No."

"I guess I'm not surprised. You would have been young when...it happened."

We fell silent, and I waited for him to open to me.

Only he didn't.

I counted to one hundred before speaking again.

"Tell me about your life there," I said, offering him a starting point.

Again, he didn't speak. Minutes passed, and when I opened my mouth to reassure him, I was silenced.

"After spending half their lives in corporate America, my parents gave up everything to join Living Light. We loved it there. We were learning to grow our own food, build our own homes, make our own clothes. We used windmills and solar panels for power. We had midwives and schoolteachers. It was the perfect escape from the harsh reality they'd left. Or so we thought."

My heart sank as Blakely relived his memories, a darkness slowly overcoming him. Briefly, I wondered if I shouldn't have pushed him. Maybe some secrets were better left buried.

"When I was ten, a new leader took control and convinced us that we must offer a sacrifice to God. He was smart, charismatic. He made everyone believe this was God's plan. He said God would reward his faithful by reviving our mortal forms so we could continue our mortal existence to spread God's word."

He shifted uncomfortably but didn't turn to face me.

"On the day it...happened...everyone was to take a small piece of bread that had been baked with poison. My parents were beginning to question the sacrifice, but it was too late. One by one, people of the community ate the pieces of bread. The poison worked quickly. It was as if they had fallen asleep. I thank God every day that it was painless for them."

He cleared his throat, sniffling.

"We were the last in line. The only others who hadn't yet taken the poison were our new leader and his daughter. Looking back," he said, shaking his head, "It must have been his plan all along. If he killed off the community members, he'd have the entire property to himself. He would own *everything*."

He turned his head as if to look at me. I reached for him, resting my hand against his back. I rubbed him through his shirt, using my free hand to wipe away my own tears for the fallen.

"Before I could take the poison, my mother slapped it out of my hand. Our leader struck her, causing my father to attack him. My mother told me to run, hide, and I did. After an hour or so, I went looking for my parents. I found their bodies. They were both dead. Our leader and his daughter were gone. I've never forgiven myself. I could have saved them. My mistake cost them their lives."

I sank to the floor beside him and straddled his lap. I held his head in my palms and stared into his murky eyes. The usual bright blue was gone.

"Listen to me," I said. "This was not your fault. You were just a child."

"I was old enough to fight back," he said, grasping my hands and pulling them down. I released his face.

"You were just a boy. You couldn't have saved them."

He stood abruptly, lifting me with him. Turning, he set me on the bed and took several steps back, not stopping until he was pressed firmly against the wall.

I considered his words. I understood his pain, his grief over surviving. Often, I'd find myself falling to my knees, screaming for an answer as to why I survived the crash. The day I decided to bury my emotions was the day I died inside.

I was broken. I was dead. Basic primal instincts were what drove my every motion.

And I didn't care...until now. Until I saw myself in another. Until I could see what suppressed emotions were really doing to me.

"I know that feeling. It's like you're falling, and you know you should try to break your fall, but you don't. You just close your eyes and focus on the rush of the wind against your cheeks."

I closed my eyes, and I could feel it; I could feel every emotion I'd once buried. They were slowly rising, slowly suffocating me. To recede back into the shadows would be an easy escape. I'd lived that way for years.

Opening my eyes, I said, "If you don't accept that maybe there was a reason you were saved, then your survivor's guilt will kill you."

"You seem to be just fine," he spat.

I winced as his words lashed me. *Fine.* Did I look fine? Maybe to those who didn't carry the baggage we carried. I knew in Blakely's eyes I was a broken girl who was struggling to overcome her demons. I knew he could see himself in me, and I was sure that terrified him.

I took a step forward, and his breath hitched. He didn't want me to close the distance between us. He didn't want me to touch him. Hell, he probably didn't want me to even look at him.

"We're the same, you and I," I said. "We're broken, but I can feel you putting my pieces back together."

I took another step forward.

"Everything feels different when I'm with you. I feel... stronger. I feel like I can face anything."

I took one more step forward. I could nearly touch him.

"Don't let your memories kill you," I said softly.

I reached forward, placing my hands flat against his chest. His heart was beating rapidly. I closed my eyes, focusing on each steady burst.

"Let them save your life," I whispered.

These same words were said to me by the priest who buried my parents, but I didn't understand them then.

I leaned forward, sliding my hands around his frame. I clasped my hands behind his back and rested my head against his chest. If it was possible, his already-erratic heartbeat increased. It screamed in my ear. I squeezed my eyes shut, replaying the many memories of my parents I'd hoped to forget.

I remembered the family dinners, the weekend movie marathons, the long drives.

I remembered the all-nighters my mom put in to help me study for an upcoming test.

I remembered the holiday traditions, the family vacations, and the long talks.

In one simple moment, the disconnect vanished, and I was flooded with the emotions I'd hoped I'd never again feel.

Tears slid down my cheeks, and I buried my face in Blakely's shirt.

Together, we'd release our demons, and we'd face the nightmares we'd been running from.

I opened my eyes, yawning. I was in bed, and the alarm on the nightstand flashed brightly. A few hours had passed since we'd admitted our past indiscretions to each other—a task neither of us had ever expected to accomplish. We'd spent the next hour or so reliving each painful memory, dusting them off and bringing them into the light of day.

I glanced over my shoulder to find Blakely curled up behind me. The length of my body was pushed up against his, and once again, I admired how perfectly we fit together.

I didn't understand those who didn't believe in fate. Meeting Blakely couldn't have been pure coincidence.

My attraction to him was immediate, but now, as I gave in to the war of emotions within me, I had to ask myself how I truly felt about him. The lust that burned within me was making way for something new, something I hadn't felt in years. I respected Blakely; hell, since the death of my parents, he was one of the few people I cared to be around.

But what did that mean? He'd admitted to me that we weren't just fucking anymore, but were we ready to label our attraction? Maybe our constant proximity and earth-shattering sex had led us to believe something more was happening. For the first time in years, I began to question my decisions I'd based on feelings.

What the hell was happening here?

I blinked away my thoughts when Blakely inhaled deeply and cleared his throat, burrowing his face into the crook of my neck. I giggled as the scruff on his chin rubbed against my skin. He smiled, and I bit my lip.

Feeling suddenly overwhelmed with the urge to kiss him, I turned around and pressed my lips to his. Soon, we were in a passionate embrace. His tongue grazed my lips, and I opened for him. With each lick, nip, and suck, he consumed me until I wasn't sure where I ended and he began.

I rolled onto him and straddled his lap, clinging tightly to his frame. His erection rubbed against me as we kissed, and

I found myself rolling my hips, relishing in each moan that escaped him. I loved the way he felt beneath me, the sounds he made, the way he offered me the control he craved.

I pulled off my top, letting it fall to the floor beside the bed. Blakely's fingers scratched at my back, and I gasped into his mouth. When his hands reached my pants, he pushed them down in a quick motion. I angled forward, letting him push them from my body completely. Nude, I remained straddling his lap as I feverishly moved my hands to unbutton his pants, freeing his erection.

Needing him inside me, I didn't waste time. I angled my hips and slid onto his length.

I gasped as he filled me completely, and slowly, I lifted myself. I repeated this process, ever so slowly, from root to tip. The exertion was minimal, yet we both had fine layers of sweat on our skin.

A low rumble escaped his chest, and I knew he needed this, needed *me*, as much as I needed it, needed him. His hands clung to me as I worked his length. My core ached as I chased my release.

My breasts rubbed against his T-shirt, and I cringed at the friction. I needed to feel him, skin on skin. As if reading my mind, he yanked off his shirt and pulled me closer. He grasped my hips, and I relinquished control to him.

Instead of viciously pounding his length into me, he maintained my pace, and his eyes never left mine. With each stroke, my heart grew heavy.

Why was he making me feel so...vulnerable?

I had never felt so exposed before, but it didn't matter. We'd escaped reality and lived in our own world. We were no longer fucking in some hotel. With each slow caress, with each deep, long kiss, with each breath taken in unison, we had left this plane and traveled to some distant, emotional existence.

Even though the thought terrified me, I didn't want him to stop. I wanted him to be there with me.

Everything in this moment felt right. With each stroke, my orgasm built inside me until I couldn't hold on to it anymore. I came hard. In long, slow waves, my release enveloped me. I cried out, James's name on my lips.

CHAPTER TWENTY-ONE

While I dressed, I was lost to my own thoughts. I was developing real feelings for my bodyguard, but I couldn't admit the words aloud. He'd made it clear that he wasn't receptive to the idea of intimacy, yet he'd yielded. Was my inability to discuss a real relationship just my subconscious saving me from the heartache of rejection? Or perhaps I was too afraid to verbally admit the walls I'd spent a great deal of time constructing were tumbling down around me.

I wondered if I'd be okay with that. Maybe it was time to truly let someone in.

Maybe it was time to finally forgive myself for my past mistakes.

"I thought we could get lunch, maybe walk around town," I said as I slipped on my sandals.

I stood, turning to face him. Summer in Maine meant hot, humid temperatures. Usually I'd opt for shorts, tank tops, and flip-flops, but since I had to be slightly more presentable at the residency, I decided on leggings, a loose top, and sandals. Blakely, on the other hand, took his job way too seriously. He wore all black—dark jeans, black T-shirt, and black shoes. Underneath it all, I was sure he was strapped, too.

"You look wicked conspicuous," I said as I scanned the length of his body. "Remember that it's summer and we're in Maine. No one is wearing all black..."

His gaze dropped as he took in his attire. "It wasn't

intentional." He shrugged. "It's fine."

I arched a brow, crossing my arms. "Honestly, James, you really should change. A heat stroke is no one's friend."

I laughed and met his gaze. His breath hitched, and time seemed to slow as he stared back at me.

"That's twice now that you've called me by my first name," he said quietly.

I hadn't even realized. His name escaped my lips naturally, as if it belonged there. Again, I was left wondering what this truly meant, what he meant. Could I acknowledge this feeling to him?

His eyes gave away nothing, so I ignored my curiosity, choosing to instead let the afternoon pass by in a daze. We strolled down Main Street, stopping to shop at independent stores. We had a late lunch at one of my favorite cafés. I gave him a tour of the university grounds, and we hiked at a nearby nature preserve.

Walking along the rocky beach, I tossed pebbles into the ocean. In this place, I felt at peace. It was as if nothing could hurt me here. I felt safe with James. I felt like the world would crumble at my feet before he'd let anything harm me.

He stood beside me, his hands shoved into his pockets as he stared out into the distance. He admired the beauty of nature, and I admired the beauty that was James Blakely. He glanced down at me and smiled. I leaned against him, and he wrapped an arm around me.

Closing my eyes, I inhaled deeply. The world smelled so familiar yet so different. It smelled of salt and sea, of trees and rain. And it smelled of James. I turned inward, snuggling against him and breathing in his essence. He always smelled of mint.

It felt like hours had passed as we stood there in silence, both knowing what needed to be said but not wanting to be the first to say it. Something had changed between us. It couldn't be love. Only characters in my novels experienced that kind of near-instant love, not real-life flesh and bone. But there was a newly formed respect between us—something that could one day grow into a strong bond like the love I'd yet to experience. *That* I knew to be true.

I didn't have to ask if James felt it, too. I knew he did. I could tell by the way he looked at me, touched me, held me close. Even though I knew of his feelings, I still questioned their meaning. I still questioned the future.

I'd lived my life without a plan, but now, with James by my side, I craved answers.

What would happen next?

When the sun began to set, we hiked back to our car—again, in silence—and drove back to town. I finally spoke when we reached the hotel and stepped into the elevator.

"You make me feel safe," I said, glancing up at him.

He frowned, never looking back at me.

"I don't think about the drama of my job or that someone's out there, watching me, when I'm with you," I said. "You make me feel...normal."

He swallowed, and I watched his Adam's apple bounce in his throat. He exhaled slowly and squeezed his eyes shut. When he opened them, he turned to face me. His bright-sapphire eyes seemed to glow as he looked at me longingly.

I leaned into him, resting a hand against his chest.

He leaned down, pressing his lips to mine. He kissed me slowly, deeply, as if he'd never again get the chance. The thought left me feeling ill, afraid. I couldn't lose him. I was finally starting to find myself again, and it was all because of him.

Someone cleared his throat, and we pulled apart to find the elevator doors open to the fifth floor and Brent Miller staring at us.

I ignored him as we exited the elevator and walked to our room to dress for tonight's formal dinner.

I pinned my hair back into an elegant bun, refreshed my makeup—opting for bold red lips—and slipped into my short black dress and strappy heels. When my look was complete, I assessed myself in the floor-length mirror. My off-the-shoulder dress reached midthigh, and the lace edging and sleeves gave the dress a sensual feel, but it wasn't too extreme. The silver cross necklace James had given me rested atop my dress, so I tucked it underneath. I gave myself a final once-over before leaving the bathroom.

James stood at the other end of the room, his gaze falling on me when I stepped out of the bathroom. I was sure I heard his breath hitch as I walked toward him. He was devastatingly gorgeous in a black suit. He looked like the man I'd interviewed—pristine, confident, undeniably sexy.

"You're stunning," he said softly.

I smiled. "You don't look so bad yourself."

He reached for me, tracing the short nail of his thumb against the curve of my cheek. "So beautiful."

I felt my cheeks heat as I looked away. I felt vulnerable under his stare. Butterflies in my stomach fluttered to life, leaving me with a tingling sensation from head to toe. Every inch of me hummed when he was near. I could no longer deny the effect James Blakely had on me. I could only hope I made him feel just as precious.

CHAPTER TWENTY-TWO

We walked, hand in hand, into the hotel's dining room. Everyone we passed stopped to stare, commenting on whatever caught his or her eye—my dress, my hand in James's, or the sex god himself. We passed the press table. I scanned the faces, offering a polite smile.

We sat at a table reserved for us and mingled with other staff members. Students were welcome to attend, but many didn't. I remembered feeling intimidated when I was a student there, so I assumed that was why the event was mainly staff and press.

We made it through the four-course meal without ruining our cover. To onlookers, we were a couple in love, but inside, I was screaming. As each second ticked by, as each person left for his or her room, we were one second closer to leaving Maine, to returning to Manhattan, to abandoning the life in which we were a couple. The closer we became, the more I realized I wanted James for more than his body, but that was never our agreement.

Another staff member made a joke, and James laughed loudly. I looked up at him, smiling. His arm was resting on the back of my chair, and I leaned into him. I scanned every inch of his face, hoping to burn the memory of this moment in my mind.

When I brought my attention back to the group, I found Margaret, the program director, staring at me. She winked, wiggling her eyebrows as her gaze darted from James to me, and I rolled my eyes. But I couldn't help the smile that formed.

"Dance with me," James whispered in my ear.

Several couples were already dancing to the slow piano number that played. I smiled as he brought me to the dance floor and rested his hands at the base of my spine. Closing my eyes, I rested my head against his chest as he held me close. The music played softly as James's steady heartbeat echoed through my mind. We didn't stop dancing, even after the song ended, and we didn't quicken our pace, even after a song too fast for slow dancing played.

We were lost in our own little world, and I was sure nothing could bring us down to reality.

But then, like any great fairy tale, something had to break up a perfect moment.

I needed to pee.

"Let me take you," he said.

I shook my head. "There's no need. Honestly, it's through the doors and down that hall. I'll be back before you even realize I'm gone."

I turned on my heel and nearly ran into Margaret.

"Oh, I'm so sorry!" I said.

"Still have two left feet, I see," Margaret joked.

I laughed and excused myself to the bathroom. When James tried to follow me, still insisting I needed an escort, Margaret stopped him, asking him to sit down and chat with her. Stuck in a web of lies, he caved, taking a seat that offered him the best view of the door I'd left through.

"I'm so glad she found you," she said as I walked out of earshot.

I shook my head, smiling. I knew Margaret would find a

way to give James *the talk*. After all, she was the closest thing I had to a mother. I liked that James was getting to know her. There were few people in my life who knew of my troubled past, and she was one of them. Once I returned to Manhattan, we would go back to simply sharing regular emails and sending holiday cards, though.

The dining room opened into the front lobby, which, thankfully, had a restroom down a nearby hallway. As I walked toward the bathroom, I felt a warm breeze brush against my skin. Glancing over my shoulder, I stared out a screen door, which led to one of the hotel's many parking lots. It was a warm night, late, and the moonlight cascaded down, offering bits of light to scare away the shadows.

After washing my hands, I fixed my makeup, re-pinned a few loose strands of hair, and turned to leave. Before I could reach the door, it opened quickly and I nearly ran into it. Stumbling, I tried to catch my fall but ended up falling backward against a stall door.

"Didn't mean to startle you," a familiar voice said.

My heart sank, fear sparking every nerve ending in my body. Slowly, I looked up, meeting the steely gray eyes staring back at me. Something was wrong. Immediately, my fight-or-flight response was on high alert. I needed to escape, to call out for help. I wasn't too far from the dining room. James could hear me...

"Don't worry, Jezebel. I have no intention of hurting you."

"Brent... What are you doing in here? This is the women's bathroom," I said, offering him an easy escape before he did something he'd regret.

My breath came in short bursts, but I didn't smell the formidable stench of alcohol on him. Even so, I assumed he was drunk.

"Well, I didn't think I'd find you in the *men's* bathroom."

He smiled, and a chill ran down my spine. The predatory gaze in his eyes made me want to vomit. He looked at me as if I were a piece of meat, as if a hunter had finally cornered his prey.

"Don't do anything stupid, Brent," I warned. "This hotel is full of people."

He laughed. "Those who aren't already in bed are drunk. Who will stop me?"

I swallowed hard. Stop him? From doing what?

"Please, Brent. Just walk away."

I was panicking. Why hadn't I ever taken self-defense courses? They would come in handy when a rapist was attacking me in a bathroom... Silently, I chastised myself for hiring a bodyguard instead of learning to protect myself.

Brent took the few small steps toward me, caging my small frame between his thick arms. He smelled of beer, shrimp, and aftershave—a nauseating combination. I turned my head away from him as he leaned into me. I kept my palms flat against his chest, hoping I could easily push him away.

He ran the tip of his nose against the curve of my ear. I listened as he inhaled slowly.

"You smell so much better than I could have ever imagined," he whispered.

His breath was hot, sticky. A slop of bile worked its way into my mouth, but I swallowed it down. I was beginning to feel light-headed; my vision blurred. I couldn't hear the laughter of people outside the bathroom walls anymore. Instead, I heard the incessant beating of my overworked heart.

Something moved out of the corner of my eye, and I felt the slightest of pinpricks against my neck as he whispered, "I told you he can't stop me."

And then, the world went black.

CHAPTER TWENTY-THREE

I woke in darkness. My mouth was dry, my lips cracked. My arms stretched above me on either side of my head, my hands bound together as I hung from the ceiling. I shifted slightly. The binding on my wrists dug into my skin, and I sucked in a sharp breath.

The world seemed...foggy. I searched my memory until everything came crashing down.

The hotel. The party. The bathroom.

Brent Miller.

He'd attacked me.

I told you he can't stop me.

I suppressed a whimper. Tears stung my eyes as I remembered the photos I'd received. Those same words were written on the back of one of the pictures I'd been sent.

My stalker.

Brent Fucking Miller.

I replayed the memory of his face repeatedly.

Who was he? I'd never heard of him, never seen him before. Was he really with the press, or was that just a cover to attend the residency?

I blinked away the tears that pooled in my eyes until they dripped down my cheeks.

The room was dark, too dark. I couldn't see anything.

Was I wearing a blindfold?

I blinked once. Twice. Nothing.

No, it was just *that* dark.

Where could he have taken me that would be *this* dark?

My mind wandered to a book I'd started to read recently. A woman's husband beat her and then left her in an underground bunker. He'd left her there to die. She'd woken just like I had—in darkness and with a foggy memory.

I wished I'd finished the book...

My neck throbbed, and I remembered the sharp pain I'd felt before the world went dark. I'd watched enough *Dexter* to know that meant he'd stuck me with a needle, drugging me into compliance.

I tried to remember something past that moment—*anything* that could tell me where I was, how many days had passed.

I was thirsty, but I'd been drinking. Was my thirst from the alcohol or a testament to the time I'd spent here?

I blinked again. Once. Twice. Still, my eyes didn't adjust to the darkness.

Did I dare call out?

What if someone was close by? This could be my only chance for survival.

I opened my mouth to speak but quickly snapped it shut.

Someone was in the room with me.

The faintest of breaths echoed in my mind. My heart seemed to escape my chest and splatter onto the floor beneath me.

He was here.

Did I dare speak? Did I dare believe I could guilt him into releasing me?

I felt the tip of a blade press against my bare back, and only then did I realize I wasn't wearing my dress. The blade slid down my skin, scratching from the base of my neck to the lowest arch of my spine. In its trail, it sliced through the strap of my bra.

Again, I tried to move my wrists, seeing if the binding would give way to a hard jerk. I clenched my jaw shut when it bit into flesh. Droplets landed on my forehead, sliding down the curves of my face before pooling in the corner of my mouth.

Blood.

Before I could decide whether it was worth it to beg for freedom, the lights turned on. I was immediately blinded. I cried out as if I'd been struck. My eyes burned, and I squeezed them shut, letting my tears wash away the sudden surge of pain. Slowly, I reopened them and locked eyes with my attacker.

"You have no idea how long I've waited for this moment," he said.

He was close, too close. He reached out, tracing the arch of my jawline. I shivered under his touch, feeling sick. Bile worked its way into my throat, and briefly, I wondered if I could use it to my advantage. If I vomited, maybe he'd leave, maybe he'd untie me to clean up, maybe he'd just let me go.

I told myself whatever lies I could think of to keep hope alive.

I needed to survive.

I wouldn't let Brent Miller be my end.

"I've been watching you for months," he said, a sly smile twisting his lips. "We met once. Of course, you'd never remember it. Blending in, staying invisible, are just a few of the ways you and I are similar. Connected."

"I remember you," I whispered.

He paused, his eyes searching mine, and then he shook his head. "I don't mean at the residency. We've met before. I saw you at the hospital that day. You were unconscious, weak, injured, yet you were so beautiful. Everyone turned to look at you when you were wheeled in. People rushed over, and I walked beside you, pretended you were mine. But I don't have to pretend anymore."

He walked toward me, a smile forming on his lips as he recalled the day that ruined my life.

"It's fate. I never believed in fate. Not until that day. My dad, he's the one. He brought us together."

I swallowed, searching his eyes. "I don't... I don't understand."

"My dad was a worthless drunk, but he was all I had. My mom never wanted us, and my dad never did anything right. Not until that day. Not until he brought me to you."

My throat was closing; my breath caught. Tears burned behind my eyes.

"Your dad was the driver. He killed my parents," I whispered.

He nodded, smiling. "I worked at the hospital. That's where I saw you. I saw them bring you in, and I knew. I could just tell. I could *feel* it."

Anger boiled in the pit of my gut, and it gave me a newfound sense of strength.

If only I could land one quick, hard hit between his legs, this would stop. I once read you could kill a man if you hit him in the balls hard enough. I wasn't sure if that was true, but I was willing to try. He came within reaching distance, and I tried to kick him.

Except, my legs failed me.

I looked down, noticing their awkward angle.

"I must wonder what you were thinking just now." He

smiled. "Were you planning to hurt me?"

Still angry, I feared what I might say, that I might upset him, so I didn't speak.

"I gave you a paralytic. Eventually you'll regain control of your legs," he said, answering my unspoken words.

More droplets of blood splattered against my skin, and I looked up. My bound arms held the weight of my body. The rope was tight, digging into my flesh. The skin of my hands was pale. I wondered how long I could stay this way before I lost my hands. If I was going to escape, I needed my hands.

Hell, I needed my legs, too.

But right now, my hands were in desperate need of blood.

I took a deep, slow breath. My throat was scratchy as I tried to speak.

"P-Please," I whispered.

"Would you like some water?" he asked.

He walked to a corner table, poured clear liquid from a pitcher into a plastic cup, and walked back to me.

"Here, let me help you," he said, angling my head back as he offered me the drink.

I considered my options. Do I swallow it down, hoping it really was water? Do I spit it out? Do I spit it at him? I decided if he wanted me drugged, he'd use his needle, so I greedily drank the liquid.

"Please," I whispered.

"More?" he asked.

"Let me go."

He smiled. "Don't waste your breath. You're not going anywhere. You see, you and I are meant to be together. Soon, you'll see that. You will," he said.

"You don't have to do this, Brent."

He closed his eyes, dragging his teeth against his bottom lip. "I love the sound of my name coming from your lips." He opened his eyes. "I don't want to force you, Jezebel. Jezebel *Tate*. I always wondered why you didn't use your real name when publishing your books. Jezebel Cox was just too cliché."

"You can let me go, and—"

"And what?" he interrupted. "And we'll be together? Out *there*? *We* don't belong out there with *them*. We're different, you and me." His eyes scanned the length of my practically nude frame. "God, you're even more gorgeous than I imagined."

He kneeled before me and ran his hand up the length of my leg. If I hadn't watched him touch my skin, I never would have known he was violating me. Silently, I thanked God for paralytics. I'd never feel him touch me. I could close my eyes and pretend I was somewhere else.

So I did just that.

I closed my eyes.

And there was James.

We were in my apartment. He smiled at me, told me I looked beautiful. The light bounced off his skin as he walked toward me.

"Jezebel."

He said my name. His lips moved, but his voice was different.

No. I needed to focus.

I wasn't here. I wasn't with *him*.

I was safe. I was with James.

He would protect me.

"*James...*" I whispered.

"Open your eyes, or I'll slice off your lids!" he screamed.

I obeyed, tears streaming down my cheeks.

"Don't ever say his name!" he said. He turned on his heel, balled his fist, and slammed it against the wall. "He doesn't *deserve* you," he said slowly.

I whimpered, staring at the floor. Only then did I notice my necklace was missing. My heart leaped. Had it fallen off? Was it nearby? Was it close enough for James to find me?

"Are you going to forget about him, Jezebel?" he asked.

I nodded.

He grabbed a handful of hair and yanked my head back. "I asked you a fucking question!"

"Y-Yes," I said between hiccups. "I-I'm sorry. I'll be g-good."

His eyes softened, and he released me. "Oh, Jezebel," he whispered. "Don't you see? Don't you see what you do to me? I can't help it. I just... I get so mad when I think about *him* touching what's *mine*, what's meant for me."

He licked his lips as he stared at me, his gray eyes growing dark.

"Your paralytic will wear off soon." He offered a toothy grin.

"P-Please, just let me go. I won't tell anyone. I swear."

He barked out a hard laugh.

"Do you think I'm an idiot? If you're out there, we'll never be together." He closed the space between us and held my face between his hands. "Don't you see? Don't you see that we're perfect for each other? I'm just like you, Jezebel. I don't want to be part of that world either."

His words bounced around my head. I'd done this to myself. I'd gotten myself into this situation. By cutting myself off from the world, I'd put a target on my back. I'd welcomed someone like Brent Miller into my world. I felt sick, and this time, I knew I wouldn't be able to stop it.

I leaned forward, expelling the liquid contents from my gut.

"Fuck. Damn it!" Brent said, taking several steps back.

The poignant odor of vomit wafted through the air. It smelled like a mix of decaying flowers and death.

Maybe now he'd move me. He'd untie my wrists and toss me aside.

But he didn't.

Instead, he left me there and walked out of the room, slamming the door behind him.

I didn't know how long I stood there, waiting, wondering if he'd come back for me or leave me to rot. I didn't know how much time passed. The pain of my hands was becoming unbearable—it was surely my brain's last-ditch effort to save my hands by making them hurt enough for me to lower them. My fingers were numb, my arms weak. I rested my head against my arm. My skin was cool, sticky. I turned my head to assess the damage. The paleness of my hands was spreading to my arms, and I knew I would soon lose them, too.

By the time Brent returned, the vomit that remained on my chin and in the corner of my mouth had caked over.

I felt disgusting, degraded. With only my underwear and broken bra, I was nearly nude, covered in filth. I couldn't move my hands, and my arms were growing stiff. As I stared at my feet, only a few inches from the pool of vomit I'd left on the floor, I noticed the black and blue marks along my ankles.

My world began to crash down around me.

Reality and self-doubt were suffocating as I began to believe I'd never survive.

"Please, let me go..." I whispered.

Save me the pain, the heartache.

"I don't want to force you, Jezebel. You need to want me as much as I want you."

He ran his hand across my stomach, and when he reached my thighs, he latched on to my core, bunching my underwear and ripping them off. The fabric dug into my skin before giving way. I cried out as he tossed the thin fabric aside.

"But if I must make you feel what I feel, then I will," he grumbled.

"Don't touch me!" I screamed.

He grabbed on to the flesh of my ass, lifting me, and tossed each leg over a shoulder. A rush of relief flooded me. The pain in my wrists eased ever so slightly, and I felt sick at the sensation.

I tried to wriggle free, but it was no use. So I screamed. I screamed as loudly as I could for as long as I could. I put everything I had into that scream, knowing it was the only weapon I had. My lungs ached, but I didn't dare stop. I wouldn't stop until I suffocated.

His fist came down on me in a quick burst. Lights danced behind my eyes, but I didn't stop screaming. His anger only fueled me more. He hit me again, but this time, I heard something crack. A sharp pain shot through my eye. I inhaled deeply, ready to make my final call, but before I could scream one last time, hands wrapped around my neck and squeezed.

My face grew hot as I struggled for air. My eyes watered and cheeks stung. With each jerk of my neck, the rope around my wrists scratched my flesh until I was certain it had reached bone. I felt the subtle jerks of my body's final attempt to grasp life until my eyelids grew heavy and my lungs ached. I stopped trying to breathe, and instead, I welcomed the darkness that was enveloping my world. My vision blurred as my eyes fluttered shut.

Suddenly, air crashed back into my lungs. The sensation was painful, burning, but I couldn't stop. I swallowed down gulps of air until the pain lessened. In the distance, I could hear voices, pounding, but my strength was depleted. I couldn't look up; instead, I hung by my wrists from the rope and stared at the ground.

Everything was beginning to hurt as the paralytic wore off.

How much more could I handle? How much would be too much? How much led to death?

I heard something break—a crash—but I didn't look up.

Two hands grasped either side of my face, and I winced, preparing to take another hit.

"Please..." I begged.

I didn't know what I was begging for—to be free, to stop the beating, to just end it... The tears that fell stung as they slid into open wounds.

"Jezebel," he said softly.

I opened my eyes to find a set of pained sapphire blues staring back at me. They burned brightly against their bloodshot cases.

"James," I whispered.

Was I dreaming?

Was I dead?

I was too weak to ask, but honestly, I didn't care.

I was with James.

I wasn't in that place anymore.

I wasn't with that monster.

I was free.

He pulled a knife from his belt and cut me down. My arms

fell forward in a limp thud. Unable to stand alone, I fell against him. He walked me over to a corner bed and set me down. He assessed my hands.

"I can't cut these off, Jezebel. You'll bleed out."

I nodded and looked at my wrists. The rope was embedded deeply.

"My hands hurt," I whispered.

"Look at me," he said as he angled my head upward. "Just stay with me, okay?"

I caught sight of a shadow behind him in time to see Brent's face directly behind James.

Before I could offer a warning, Brent brought down a knife, stabbing James in the shoulder. Releasing me, James spun on his heel, reached back, yanked the knife free, and slashed it forward. He sliced through Brent's shirt, and a thin red line blotched the dirty fabric.

I tried to run, but my legs gave out after just a few steps, and I tumbled to the floor. James glanced over at me, and Brent took advantage of his distraction. He landed several hits before James had the chance to strike back.

Across the room, I saw Brent's suit coat, a holstered handgun sticking out of its inner pocket. It felt like an eternity had passed by the time I'd finally crawled to it. I grabbed on to the jacket and yanked it down, and the chair fell over beside me. My fingers ached as I slid the gun from its holster. I pushed myself off the ground and leaned against the wall, pointing the gun at the two men.

"Stop!" I yelled, but no one listened.

I tried to pull the trigger, but my hands were too weak. I tried again. The trigger gave way, but I couldn't pull it back hard enough to release a bullet. A sharp pain shot through my hand and down my arm, and I nearly dropped the weapon.

In a movement too quick for my swollen eyes, Brent fell to the ground, retrieved a hidden pistol from his ankle, and pointed it at James.

A rush of adrenaline soared through me. Screaming, I pulled the trigger, emptying the clip in Brent's direction, hoping at least one bullet would hit.

The room fell silent. Dropping the empty pistol, I crawled over to their bodies, reaching Brent's first. Lying in a pool of blood, he remained motionless as I shimmied past him.

"James?" I whispered.

My voice cracked. I collapsed by his side and stared down at him. His shirt was stained red, but he was breathing.

"James?"

Tears pooled at the outer creases of his eyes as he glanced at me.

"Stay with me," I said.

My eyes were heavy, and my chest ached. I fought to escape the darkness that was threatening to consume me. I rested my head on James's chest. His shirt was hot, sticky, and it clung to my cheek. His usually steady, strong heartbeat was weak.

Th-Thump.

Th-Thump.

Thump.

Thump.

Th...

I focused on James's heartbeat until I couldn't hear anything anymore.

CHAPTER TWENTY-FOUR

I knew I was in a hospital before I even opened my eyes. I could smell it, hear it. The sterile room I was sure I was lying in smelled of chemicals—specifically, bleach. And it was nauseating. The incessant beeping of my monitors rang at volumes too high for someone just waking up. I wasn't sure how long I'd been asleep, but I felt like I wasn't ready to embrace the world.

Because I remembered everything.

I was sure that wasn't normal. In the movies, people waking up in a hospital always had some form of amnesia, and that saved them from the heartache of having a memory.

But that was my curse. My impeccable memory that never spared me.

As soon as the grogginess started to fade and I could open my eyes, I remembered what had happened.

I remembered being taken from the hotel.

I remembered being beaten by Brent Miller.

I remembered shooting the gun.

I remembered listening to James's heartbeat until I couldn't anymore.

I remembered everything Tara said to me each time she visited.

But I don't remember how I got from that room to here.

And I don't remember James visiting me.

Had he survived?

"Jezebel? Can you hear me?" Tara asked. "Nurse. Nurse! I think she's waking up."

Fuck.

I'd hoped it wasn't obvious.

I didn't want to deal.

I couldn't deal.

I wanted to escape the torment that was rehabilitation by keeping my eyes closed forever.

But I couldn't. I had to face the world.

Slowly, I opened my eyes. The light was bright, blinding, and it bounced off the white walls and ceilings.

"Can we dim the lights?" Tara asked.

The lights went out, and I sucked in a quick burst of air. I was in darkness again, and I wasn't alone. I could feel eyes on me, watching, waiting, lingering just an arm's length away. My heart raced, and my mind was spinning.

"Turn them back on!" I screamed.

I was blinded again, but anything was better than suffocating in darkness.

I scanned the room, swallowing the knot that had formed in my throat. Tara stood by my side, and a nurse was by the door.

"James?" I whispered.

My voice cracked, my throat dry. It hurt to speak, but I needed to know if he had survived.

Tara shushed me. "Don't worry about him right now. We need to focus on you."

Tears threatened to spill. "Is h-he dead?"

"Jezebel," a familiar voice said.

I looked over to find James standing in the doorway. He dropped the two cups he was holding. They crashed to the floor, sending a slop of coffee in every direction. Ignoring the nurse's protests, he walked through the mess, leaving a trail of brown footprints from the door to my bed.

"James," I whispered.

My heart ached for him as I watched him walk toward me. The bright lights of the hospital room cast an eerie glow around him; it was as if he was surrounded by a white light.

"They said you might never wake up," he said softly.

"I thought you…"

I shook my head, tears spilling. My throat clenched as I sobbed, making it hard to speak, to breathe, to think about the man before me.

When he reached my side, he grasped my hand in his, bringing it to his mouth, placing a soft kiss on the skin.

That was when I noticed the damage.

I held my arms before me, examining the scars that encircled my wrists.

"Ms. Tate?" a woman's voice said. "I'm Doctor Patel, your attending physician."

By the time I finally tore my eyes from my wrists, she had already scribbled something onto her clipboard. She pressed a few buttons on the machines surrounding my bed and wrote down more notes. When she was finished, she slid her pen into the pocket of her white lab coat and smiled at me.

"Can you tell me your full name?" she asked.

"My throat," I said. I reached for my neck.

She nodded, looking at the nurse, who had busied herself by cleaning up the mess James had left. "Get her some ice chips."

The nurse quickly left the room.

"I know it's disorienting, but I need you to answer my

questions. Do you think you can do that?"

I shook my head. "It hurts."

I grasped my neck, and Brent Miller flashed before my eyes. I gasped as I felt his fingers clench my neck in his feeble attempt to stop my screams. Quickly, I dropped my arms, letting them fall to my lap.

The nurse returned with a clear plastic cup of ice chips. After handing the cup to me, she continued cleaning the mess on the floor.

"That should help," the doctor said as I sucked an ice cube into my mouth.

"Why can't she have water?" Tara asked.

"She can soon, but she's just woken up. Her stomach needs to settle. We need to cover some things first, and we'd like to control her intake for now."

The frozen chips melted in my mouth, turning to cool liquid that coated my throat as I swallowed it down. The pain lessened, but it was just a tease. The ice chips weren't enough. I needed at least a gallon of water to soothe my dry, scratchy throat.

"Can you tell me your full name, please?" the doctor asked.

I answered.

"Do you know where you are?"

I told her I was in a hospital, but I didn't know where.

"You're still in Portland, Maine," she answered.

"How long?" I whispered.

"You've been in a coma for nearly three months."

Three months. I'd been asleep for *three* months. Brent Miller had stolen three months of my life. I was grateful to be alive, to know that James was alive, but I couldn't help the growing feeling of hatred forming within me. I hated Brent Miller for ruining my life. I hated him for taking time away from me—time I could never get back.

"How are you feeling?" the doctor asked when I finally looked at her.

She was pretty, petite. Her black hair was tied back, but strands fell into her eyes each time she looked down at me.

"I don't know," I said honestly.

She nodded. "Confusion is common. Are you experiencing any pain right now?"

Looking at my wrists, I thought about her question. My hands, wrists, and arms were covered in fine, white scars.

I shook my head. "I don't think so."

"Good. You've healed quickly and well, and you shouldn't experience any more pain in your wrists."

My vision began to blur as tears threatened to spill.

"What happened?" I asked.

I remembered everything Brent did to me, but I didn't remember getting to the hospital.

"When you were brought in, you were already unconscious. You had slipped into a coma, which is common in cases like yours. Your body and mind were under extreme duress. You lost a lot of blood, and there was trauma."

"Trauma?" I asked.

"At some point, you hit your head, which caused some swelling and breaks. When this happens, the brain can temporarily lose its ability to control awareness and arousal. Shutting down is a way the body copes with extreme situations."

I swallowed hard, cringing at the burning sensation in my throat.

"You were in surgery to remove the binding and repair

the tissue damage. We saved what we could, but we did need to remove some dead tissue."

"Will I be able to do things...normally?" I asked.

Tara sat on the edge of my bed and grabbed my hand, giving me a reassuring squeeze. But she never looked at me. My breath hitched as I waited for the doctor to answer.

"Only time will tell. We were able to save enough tissue to prevent the injury from affecting your day-to-day use of your hands, and we will be monitoring your brain function during the rest of your stay here. At this point, we're unsure if you'll have any long-term damage because of your head injuries. You're lucky, Ms. Tate. Your injuries were severe enough to become more than a cosmetic issue."

I nodded, swallowing down more tears. She was right. I was lucky to be alive. It shouldn't matter that I'd lost three months. I had my future, and I was finally free. That was what mattered.

"Wh-Where is he? Did...did he survive?" I stuttered.

"Ms. Tate, you really shouldn't worry about anything but your recovery. Your body may have healed, but you need to work on your mind, too."

"Just tell me!" I shouted with a force too great for my aching throat, causing a surge of pain to shoot through me. Nurses walking outside my room stopped and looked over, but I didn't care. "Just tell me if he's still out there," I added more quietly.

"He's dead," James said. He reached forward, tucking my hair behind my ear.

A sense of relief flooded me; it was a feeling I'd never experienced. Knowing he was gone, I felt safe, free, alive. I'd never celebrated the death of another human being, but knowing he was gone made me feel...happy, at ease.

"The police will want to speak with you," Tara said. "They checked in fairly regularly during the first month..."

I nodded.

"It can wait until she's discharged," James said.

"No, I want to get it over with. Tell them to come today."

Tara nodded. "I'll make the call." She left the room, busily typing buttons on her cell phone.

"When can I go home?" I asked the doctor.

"I'd like to keep you for observation—"

"When?" I interrupted.

"Another couple of days. For now, I'd like you to relax, but if you need anything, just press this button," she said as she motioned to a remote on my bedside table. "That will also control your bed and the television."

I nodded, thanking her, and she left. I was alone with James.

"Don't be nervous," he said.

I shook my head. "I'm not. I just want this over with."

He smiled down at me.

"How are you?" I asked, letting my eyes scan the length of his body.

He looked tired, weak. His usually tan skin was pale. Dark circles were painted beneath his muddled blue eyes. He looked as if he hadn't slept in months.

"I'm fine."

"You were injured," I said.

"Don't worry about me, Jezebel."

"Damn it, James. I'm not a child!" I grabbed the bedside controller and pressed the button so I could sit up in bed. "I need to know what happened."

"But we don't need to talk about it *now*."

"Now seems like the perfect time since the police will soon be here," I countered.

He didn't speak.

"You were shot," I said, replaying that night in my mind. "I remember everything. I shot Brent, I crawled to you, and I listened to your heartbeat until I couldn't hear it anymore."

"It was too much on your system. You fell unconscious," he said.

"Please, James. I need to know."

He exhaled slowly. "I was tracking your location, but the necklace told me you hadn't left the area. It didn't make sense. I tore apart every room searching for you, but you weren't there. When I couldn't find you, I went to neighboring houses. He kept you in one of the basements. He'd killed the elderly woman who'd lived there."

"Oh, God," I sobbed.

"She didn't suffer. Honestly, it didn't seem like he'd even planned it. I believe he attacked out of passion, which derailed any previous plans he'd made to take you. We got lucky. His inability to wait for an opportune time worked to our advantage, because since we'd been searching for you, the police were everywhere. They heard the fighting, gun shots, and they found us."

"And you're okay? You're *really* okay?" I whispered.

He nodded and brought his hand to his chest. "I never even lost consciousness, and now, it's just a scar."

My head fell into my palms as I released everything I had pent up inside me. The bed squeaked as James sat beside me and rubbed my back. I leaned against him, closing my eyes.

I didn't know how long Brent had kept me prisoner. I

didn't know what would happen next. But I'd survived. I hadn't given up. And now, it was over. It was *finally* over. My stalker was gone. He couldn't hurt me anymore.

Even after my tears dried, I remained curled up beside James. I didn't move until the police arrived.

"Ms. Tate? I'm Detective Young," a man said as he flashed me his badge. "How are you feeling?"

"Tired," I said. A truthful, yet ironic, response.

"I'm glad you're doing well. I've stopped by a few times to see how you were doing," Detective Young said, smiling.

I offered a half smile, but inside, I wanted to escape, to forget everything, to pretend I'd never gone to Maine.

"I'd like to ask you a few questions regarding your kidnapping and the subsequent death of Mr. Miller. Do you feel up to it? I can come back if you're not well enough."

"No, I'm fine. I can answer your questions now."

I shifted in the bed and tried to sit up as much as possible. My wounds had healed, but sleeping for three months had left me stiff. My joints ached every time I moved.

"I'd like to record our conversation. Is that okay with you?" he asked.

I shrugged. "I guess."

He pulled out a thin, black tape recorder from his suit jacket pocket and placed it on the overbed table. He pressed a button to record and asked me to recount everything I could remember. James, ever faithful, remained by my side. Sliding his fingers between mine, he held my hand, offering reassuring squeezes whenever my memories became hard to bear.

"Had you ever seen him before?" he asked.

I shook my head. "H-He said we'd met, but I don't remember it. He said I wouldn't. He said our ability to stay invisible made us...connected." I shuddered at the thought.

"Thank you, Ms. Tate. I'm sorry if recounting this has been difficult for you," he said, shutting off the recorder and sliding it back into his pocket.

I shook my head. "It's fine. I just want this nightmare over with."

"Of course," he said, pulling a business card from his pocket. "If you remember anything else, you can call me at any time."

"I'll take that," James said. "You should already have our information. We'll be returning to Manhattan as soon as she's released."

"Yes, understandable."

"Are you going to file charges?" Tara asked.

I hadn't even noticed she'd returned to the room after contacting the police.

The detective shook his head. "No, ma'am. This was a clear case of self-defense."

Not realizing I'd been holding my breath, I exhaled slowly.

CHAPTER TWENTY-FIVE

The next couple of days passed in a blur. The nurses checked on me every hour to make sure I hadn't fallen back into a coma. Apparently that was a major concern. When Doctor Patel finally cleared me, I nearly jumped for joy. I would have walked out in the hospital gown if I wasn't afraid of mooning everyone I passed.

The ride back to Manhattan was silent. Every few minutes, James would glance over at me or reach for me in some way. I was sure he was just reminding me that he was there, that I was safe. I'd smile at him or hold his hand. It was a show, of course, because internally, I was an empty void. I was shutting down again. Only this time, I was aware of it. I knew the signs. Avoiding my feelings had kept me safe...until it didn't anymore.

When we reached my Manhattan brownstone, James parked, grabbed our bags, and helped me into the apartment. My muscles were still stiff, but after a few long soaks in my hot tub and a regular workout routine, I'd be back to normal, according to my doctor. Physically, anyway. Emotionally, I was shattered. That's what happens when a broken person breaks. She shatters.

I took the first step into my apartment and looked around. Everything was where I'd left it. The window curtains were drawn shut to keep out prying eyes. The lights were off. The fruit on the counter was moldy. If I'd opened the fridge, I'd find the food had spoiled. My apartment was the physical representation of what I'd become. Dead.

When I was asleep in my coma, the world stopped moving. But really, that didn't happen. The world kept going on, kept living its life as if nothing out of the ordinary had changed.

But everything had changed.

I swallowed hard, turned, and faced James.

"I have to see someone," I said.

He nodded, understanding my need. "I've been doing some research. I found someone who specializes in trauma victims."

He pulled out his phone, pressed a few buttons, and handed it to me. Her website flashed back at me. I clicked on the About page and read her bio. She had experience working with celebrities and specialized in treating the trauma associated with fame. I scanned the page, settling on the final message.

Don't wait until it's too late.

"I've already contacted her. She wants to help. Her mobile number is in my contacts."

I should have been angry with him. Had Tara done this when my parents died, I would have never forgiven her betrayal. After all, I was young, naïve. I'd truly believed I could handle it on my own. I'd truly believed spilling my contents to a shrink made me weak.

But I'd been wrong.

I closed his phone's browser and navigated to his contacts. Her number was the first number listed.

She answered after just one ring.

"Doctor Scott."

She was loud, forceful, confident.

"This is Jezebel Tate. I... I need help."

"Jezebel, I'm so glad you called. I've spoken to Mr. Blakely about your situation. How are you?"

How was I? I was tired of being asked how I was. I was tired of staring at pained expressions of guilt over what happened to me, but most importantly, I was tired of lying. I was tired of hiding.

"I'm breaking," I whispered.

"Jezebel... Is it okay if I call you Jezebel?" she asked.

I nodded, sniffling.

"Hello?" she said.

I cleared my throat. "Yes, sorry. It's fine."

"How about you call me Beatrice?"

"Okay," I whispered.

"Jezebel, I know it seems like your world is crumbling around you, but it's not. I promise you will get through this. I promise I will help get you through this."

I didn't say anything.

"Say it with me Jezebel. Stop telling yourself lies. You will get through this."

"I will get through this," I repeated. My voice was weak, shaky.

"I'd like to see you tomorrow morning. Are you available at eight?"

"Yes," I said.

"Very good. Jezebel, are you alone tonight? Or is there someone who can stay with you?"

I glanced at James. "I have someone who will stay with me."

He smiled at me.

"Okay. I'll see you tomorrow morning."

"I'll see you then."

"Jezebel?"

"Yes?"

"Never forget that you're stronger than you could ever imagine."

★ ★ ★

I stripped and stared at myself in the floor-length mirror. I didn't recognize the girl who stared back at me. My chocolate-brown eyes and hair seemed...dull, faded, muddled. My skin was pale, my frame gaunt. I'd lost weight and muscle when I was in the coma.

I stared at my hands. A ring of scar tissue encircled both wrists. I turned them over, staring at my palms. I'd lost tissue on a few fingers, and now the craters in my skin mocked me.

"Jezebel?" James said, knocking on my door.

He found me standing nude before my mirror, staring at my imperfections. Stepping behind me, he wrapped his arms around me, holding me close. I looked back, and he placed a soft kiss to my temple.

"You're beautiful," he whispered.

I closed my eyes and let his words envelop me.

Beautiful.

"You should finish getting ready," he said, stepping back and handing me my swimsuit.

I dressed quickly and let him lead me into the living room. Slowly, I climbed the stairs to my rooftop deck. Reaching the hot tub, I tossed my towel aside and got in, letting the heat of the water soothe my aching joints.

James moved to sit behind me, and I leaned against his

long, muscular frame as he massaged the kinks from my underused body. I stared at the sky and imagined I could see the stars.

I thought about this place and about James. I'd called Manhattan home for many years now, and I'd always felt safe here. Now that Brent was gone, James didn't have a reason to stay. The allure of Manhattan no longer existed. I wasn't pulled to it the way I had been. Instead, I was pulled to James—to a life with him, to the safety I felt when in his arms.

But was he pulled to me, too?

"Will you stay with me?" I asked.

James leaned forward, wrapping his arms around me and squeezing tightly.

"Always," he said, his breath hot on my neck.

I smiled, wrapped my arms around his, and closed my eyes.

Tomorrow, I would see Doctor Scott.

I would face my demons.

I would confront the lies I'd kept, the lies that had haunted me all these years.

In time, with James by my side, even the shattered pieces of me would mend my fractured soul.

EPILOGUE

Today marked one year since Jezebel asked me to stay with her. She had asked me as if I had another option. But I hadn't. After all we'd been through in the short time I'd known her, I was addicted. She was like no one I'd ever known.

Sometimes, she would lean against me and wrap my arm around her waist. She'd look up at me with doe eyes, innocent, frightened. In those moments, I knew she was reliving her past.

She was reliving the moments I broke my promise to her.

I told her I would keep her safe, shield her from the dangers of this world. I'd even believed it myself. But in the seconds that led up to her abduction, I was a fool. I'd given in to the facade we'd paraded before her friends. I'd let myself believe we were safe, together, happy.

And my idiocy nearly cost Jezebel her life.

It's been a year since Jezebel broke down her walls and asked for help. She looked to me for strength. She didn't realize she was the strongest person I knew. To ask for my strength, as if I were the strong one, was ludicrous.

She had agreed to see Doctor Scott three times a week until the pain lessened and she learned to forgive herself for her role in her abduction and her parents' death. I admired her for facing her demons. If only I were that strong.

"You're staring at me," she said, smiling. She glanced up at me. "Why?"

"Your beauty leaves me awestruck."

Her cheeks flushed and dimples formed. Even in her most casual of moments, she was heart-stopping.

After each session with Doctor Scott, she asked me why I too wouldn't face my demons. In those moments, her grace melted into a distracting form of courage that left me breathless.

I never knew what to tell her.

Unlike Jezebel, I'd chosen to run away, to let them die.

Unlike Jezebel, I'd killed my parents.

Unlike Jezebel, who effortlessly released her secrets to me, I refused to relinquish my truth, for the cost of knowing was but mine to bear.

Unlike Jezebel, I would live with my mistakes until I took them to my grave.

My parents weren't the victims of a drunk driver; they were the victims of systemic manipulation.

Even in the end, even when I saw the oppression for what it was, I yielded.

Jezebel believed we were destined to meet, to help each other, but I wasn't so sure.

Could there be help for the damned? For the wicked?

At times, when the darkness had been too much to bear, I'd considered leaving her. I knew she was better off without me. I was weak; I'd never been anything more.

When I brought her home from Maine, the light that initially drew me to her had faded. When we first met, she took my breath away. I'd never met someone who had been equally heart-stopping and frustrating. Her naïveté diminished after spending just a few days together.

But as I looked at her now, I saw that light returning.

How could I tell her there was no hope for me? How could I knowingly smother the spark that diminished her shadows?

Habitually, I locked the door behind me, setting the alarm as Jezebel tossed her bag onto the island counter. Even with Brent Miller dead, I still routinely checked the apartment. In the hospital, I'd told her she was safe now, and there was nothing I wouldn't give to ensure I kept that promise.

"James?"

Internally, I smiled.

After we'd begun to admit what our relationship was becoming, she started calling me by my first name, not last. Each time my name left her lips, a shiver shot through me. I was sure my hair stood on end and that everyone around us could tell she had become something more.

"Hmm?" I replied, turning to face her.

She stepped beside me, looping her hands around my waist.

Even now, dressed casually after a day of appointments, shopping, and lunch, she was stunning. Her hair hung in soft curls around her shoulders, and her chocolate-brown eyes were shining brightly.

It was then that I saw it. It took a year of wondering how long it would take Doctor Scott to take Jezebel's shattered pieces and put them back together. The woman I'd once known was staring back at me, her eyes devious glints sparkling like whiskey in the moonlight.

She gazed up at me, her lips curving into a sly smile. I felt the sensation resonate deep within me. I clenched my jaw shut, fighting the erection that inevitably came whenever she gave me her come-fuck-me eyes.

The last time I touched her, we connected in a way that

left me raw. It wasn't about fucking or her orgasm. It was about a connection between two people, the feeling of her skin brushing against mine. Something formed between us and forced us into admission.

The last time I touched her, we were still happy. I hadn't let my guard down, I hadn't lost her to *him*. In the year since, every night, I held her in my arms while she fell asleep because she couldn't sleep alone anymore. When she woke up screaming, sure he had returned for her, I was gutted. I hated that I could protect her body but I couldn't protect her mind. Instead, I had to trust that Doctor Scott would keep that safe. Trusting Jezebel's well-being in the hands of another was one of the hardest obstacles I'd had to face.

She stood on her tiptoes and brushed her lips against mine. Closing her eyes, she kissed me. What started as a slow, deep, longing kiss turned more fervent as each second ticked by.

She bunched my cotton shirt into the palm of her hands and pulled me down. I ran a hand through her locks, grabbing the hair at her scalp and tugging playfully, relishing the feeling of her soft strands tickling the sensitive skin between my fingers. She smiled against my lips.

Slipping her hands beneath my shirt, she teased my muscles, scratching the skin until she reached my shoulders. She pulled my shirt over my head and dropped it onto the floor.

"Maybe we shouldn't," I said.

Had I pushed her? Had I hinted that I wanted her before she was ready?

"I want to," she whispered. "I'm ready."

She looked up at me, dragging her teeth against her bottom lip. The skin reddened, forming a suckable plumpness that made me groan in response. The smallest of movements left me drunk on her scent.

I pulled her into my arms and carried her into the bedroom, setting her down on the bed. She freed her arms from her dress, shimmying free and letting the fabric fall to the ground. Nude, vulnerable, raw, beautiful, she sat before me, motioning me toward her.

The attack had left her feeling damaged, unfixable, ugly, but that was far from the truth. Jezebel was a rare treasure, a coveted beauty, and not a day passed when I didn't thank God for her.

I dropped my pants and briefs and watched as she scooted back so her head was resting against my pillow. On my hands and knees, I crawled toward her, liberally placing wet kisses against her exposed skin. Devouring every inch of her, I kissed, licked, and sucked her skin until she moaned my name.

I pulled her into a long, slow kiss as I slid into her. She was tight, her skin scorching compared to my own. She angled her hips, linking her legs around my back, and I sank deeper. Resting my forehead against hers, I closed my eyes and focused on the feeling of her heart pounding against my chest, of her breath hitching in her throat, of her nails scratching against the skin of my back.

There was an unintentional rhythm to the way she and I had sex, to the way she fit against me. I'd never believed in fate, but after mere weeks of being her bodyguard, I'd begun to wonder if I should've.

I opened my eyes and stared down at her. In all the times I'd been with her, she'd never relinquished control so completely. She liked to be on top, to be dominant in her most intimate of moments, and I was okay with that. I'd given her what she desired every time I'd touched her.

But today, as she lay on the bed, inviting me in, she submitted to me.

She reached for me, running a hand through my hair. Her skin was flushed, her eyes glossy. We were both breathless, sweaty, tired, but the idea of disconnecting was too hard to bear. With each kiss, with each caress, she told me she needed me. But in truth, she didn't.

Her demons had already released her, while mine still clung tightly, pulling me into a suffocating grasp. And as Jezebel opened herself to me in ways she'd never done before, I could only hope the demons of my past would release me, too...if only for tonight.

Continue the Pieces of Me Duet with Book Two

Truth We Bear

Keep reading for an excerpt!

EXCERPT FROM *TRUTH WE BEAR*
BOOK TWO IN THE PIECES OF ME DUET

I loved the way her nose crinkled when she was choosing the perfect color. I loved the way her brows furrowed when she was concentrating on the next stroke. I loved the way she sighed when it all came together. But most of all, I loved that she was painting again.

It had taken countless nights of lost sleep, appointments with a celebrity guru therapist, and more than a year's time, but Jezebel was slowly becoming her former self: the quick-witted, smart-talking woman I'd fallen in love with despite my every effort not to.

The locks clicked closed, and I typed in the security password on the alarm system. I smiled internally, thinking about the day I'd installed the system. She had insisted we choose 1-2-3-4-5-6 as the password. Her reasoning? Because it was ridiculous. No one would try it. I shook my head, suppressing a chuckle.

Apartments in New York City were small, but Jezebel had managed to score the perfect place with this brownstone. She loved it. I could tell by the look on her face when she'd offered me a tour of my new home. As her bodyguard, I had been hired to protect her from a stalker, and part of the deal was that I lived with her until he was caught.

Brent Miller.

Brent Fucking Miller.

His name made my veins ice. I exhaled slowly, my fists squeezed at my sides. I hated him, but I hated myself most of all. I'd promised her I'd protect her from him, and even though he'd met his fate, I still hated knowing he'd gotten as close to her as he had.

I shrugged off my jacket and folded it over the back of the barstool chair by the kitchen counter. Without a formal dining area, we often ate here. Jezebel once teased that, in time, we'd do other—much naughtier—things on this very counter.

But that was before.

Before Brent Miller abducted her.

Before Brent Miller nearly raped her.

Before Brent Miller wormed his way into her soul, burrowing deeply, forever changing her.

For many months after her return to me, she'd slept in the bedroom closet. I'd slept upright, my back to the wall beside the closed and locked door between us, my gun in its holster, clipped to my pants. She'd never admitted it, but she'd feared being alone with me while she slept. She'd feared being alone with *anyone* while she'd slept, so I'd installed a lock on her closet door, and she'd kept the world at bay, sleeping with the door locked and the light on.

After several months, she'd slowly emerged from the closet, returning to her bed. I'd remained on the floor, but this time, I'd positioned myself between her and the bedroom door. After a few weeks, I'd woken to find her nestled beside me, her head on my lap, shivering without a blanket. I'd carried her to bed, tucking her in. Before I could return to the floor, she'd woken, grabbed my hand, and beckoned me to sleep beside her.

A year after Jezebel's abduction, I'd begun to see the brazen woman I fell in love with. There was a spark in her eyes, in the way she watched me move. I'd find her gnawing her lower lip, her eyes trailing my frame. I was terrified of returning those glances. While I yearned to touch her again, the thought of rushing her recovery made me feel ill.

We'd had sex exactly one time since her abduction, and it was like nothing we'd ever experienced before. Usually a take-charge woman, she'd offered me the reins, and slowly, I'd made love to her. I'd touched her softly, sweetly. I'd kissed the scars *he* had left on her. But that was weeks ago.

Usually, she painted in the spare bedroom, which served as her writing office and art studio, but today, sprawled on the floor, paint swatches scattered about, she was in the living room. She glanced up, smiling.

"I smell Chinese," she said, inhaling dramatically. She stood, wiping her hands together as she trudged toward me.

"Chicken Mei Fun," I said, pulling out the carton of noodles from the bag. Her eyes lit up, just as I knew they would. It didn't take me long to learn her favorites from every local restaurant. Jezebel was a habitual eater, and that made my job as her bodyguard much easier. "And spring rolls with extra sauce on the side."

She exhaled sharply, her hand over her chest as she squeezed her eyes shut. "A man after my heart."

I arched a brow. "I thought I already had that."

She smiled widely, closing the space between us. Standing on her tiptoes, she placed a gentle kiss to my lips before turning on her heels to face what she really wanted: dinner.

"Chopsticks? Score!"

"No plates tonight?" I asked, already knowing the answer.

She shook her head, turning toward the sink to wash her hands. I grabbed two wineglasses, poured generous splashes into each one, and carried them to the living room.

"How was work?" she asked as I set up our dinner on the coffee table.

"Good. I think I've found some temporary bodyguard work in the city."

"Really? That's great! Where?" she asked as she dried her hands with a towel. She hung it on its hook and walked toward me.

"There's a small startup that's looking for experienced guards. They cater to celebrities and the wealthy staying in the city short-term. New York is perfect for this kind of work."

She smiled. I knew saying that would make her happy. When she hired me, we'd talked about moving, but she loved Manhattan. Even though she'd known it was risky, her stubbornness had prevailed; she would not move. Now that that fucker was gone for good, she would breathe easier, and I could start settling down in the city. While I was still technically her bodyguard, she didn't really need my services anymore. And if I had to sit through another weekday *Gilmore Girls* marathon with her, I'd go crazy, so I'd started looking for work that would get me out of the house while not keeping me too far away from Jezebel.

She flopped onto the couch beside me and slurped her noodles from her chopsticks. Jezebel was a food junkie. She could dive into her meal and completely finish before ever realizing she'd forgotten to turn on the TV, which, let's be honest, was the whole point of eating in the living room. I suppressed a smile after she moaned while eating.

I turned on the TV and froze in fear when I saw the news headline.

As a marine and as a bodyguard, I'd often faced dire circumstances. My decisions had resulted in loss of life. But rarely had I ever felt that feeling of utter dread when your heart seemingly stops beating yet your blood is rushing to your head. That moment of complete shock and fear when you know your world is about to end and all you can do is sit and watch it happen.

But I felt it now.

"Once again, for those just tuning in, two bodies have been found deep in the woods. Witnesses discovered the graves while hiking pine plantations near Morgan Hill State Park in upstate New York. More on this breaking story…"

My chest clenched, and I felt like I was really, truly dying. I'd come close to dying before, and my career wasn't exactly gentle on my soul, but I'd never feared death. Then again, I'd never feared life either.

"You okay, babe?" Jezebel asked.

I swallowed the knot in my throat and nodded. "Piece of chicken lodged in my throat. I'm okay."

She rubbed my back, trying to soothe my pain. I loved her caring nature. She was a spitfire most times, and it was rare when she showed how gentle a soul she actually was. But now, in this moment, I fought the urge to slap away her hand. Not because I wanted to but because I wasn't sure I could lie if she asked one more time.

This story continues in book two of the Pieces of Me Duet
Truth We Bear!

ALSO BY DANIELLE ROSE

Pieces of Me Duet:

Lies We Keep

Truth We Bear

**For a full list of Danielle's other titles,
visit her at DRoseAuthor.com**

ACKNOWLEDGMENTS

Writing is a team sport, and I couldn't have released this book without the assistance of a select group of people:

To my amazing publisher, Waterhouse Press—thank you for believing in me and the many worlds that clutter my mind.

To Scott, my editor—thank you so much for your words of wisdom. This is a much better story because of you.

To Robin and Tara—you've both sacrificed so much to make the early versions of this book possible. I hope you know your tireless effort never went unnoticed.

To my readers—I get to do what I love because of you. Thank you.

ABOUT DANIELLE ROSE

Dubbed a "triple threat" by readers, Danielle Rose dabbles in many genres, including urban fantasy, suspense, and romance. The *USA Today* bestselling author holds a Master of Fine Arts in creative writing from the University of Southern Maine.

Danielle is a self-professed sufferer of 'philes and an Oxford comma enthusiast. She prefers solitude to crowds, animals to people, four seasons to hellfire, Nature to cities, and traveling as often as she breathes.

Visit her at DRoseAuthor.com